Dick Presco

Dick Prescotts's Fourth Year at West Point

by H. Irving Hancock

CHAPTER I

DICK REPORTS A BROTHER CADET

"Detachment halt!" commanded the engineer officer in charge.

Out on the North Dock at West Point the column of cadets had marched, and now, at the word, came to an abrupt stop.

This detachment, made up of members of the first and third classes in the United States Military Academy, was out on this August forenoon for instruction in actual military engineering.

The task, which must be accomplished in a scant two hours, was to lay a pontoon bridge across an indentation of the Hudson River, this indentation being a few hundred feet across, and representing, in theory, an unfordable river.

"Mr. Prescott!"

Cadet Richard Prescott, now a first classman, and captain of one of the six cadet companies, stepped forward, saluting.

"You will build the bridge today, Mr. Prescott, continued the instructor, Lieutenant Armstrong, Corps of Engineers, United States Army.

"Very good, sir," replied Dick.

With a second salute, which was returned, Prescott turned to divide his command rapidly into smaller detachments.

It was work over which not a moment of time could be lost. All must be done with the greatest possible despatch, and a real bridge was called for—-not a toy affair or a half-way experiment.

"Mr. Holmes," directed Prescott, "you will take charge of the boats. Mr. Jordan, take charge of the balk carriers!"

A balk is a heavy timber, used, in this case, in the construction of the pontoon.

Cadet Jordan, one of the biggest men, physically, in the first class, scowled as he received this order for what was especially arduous duty.

"That's mean of you, Prescott," glowered Jordan.

"If you have any complaints to make, sir, make them to the instructor," return Cadet Captain Prescott, after a swift, astonished look at his classmate.

"You know I can't do that," muttered Cadet Jordan. "But you———"

"Silence, sir, and attend to your duty!"

Then, raising his voice to one of general command, Prescott called:

"Construct the bridge!"

Jordan fell back, with a surly face and a muttered imprecation, to take command of the squad of yearlings, or third classman who must serve in carrying the heavy balks.

In the meantime Dick's roommate, Greg Holmes, had hurried his squad away to the flat-bottomed, square-ended pontoon boats, placing his crews therein.

Almost instantly, it seemed, Greg had placed the first boat in position.

"Lay the balks!" ordered Dick Prescott.

Cadet Jordan moved forward with some of his yearlings, who carried the heavy balks, or flooring timbers, on their shoulders. It was hot, hard work—- "thankless," as the young men often termed it in private.

These balks were laid across the first pontoon.

As quickly as the balks had been laid the detachment of lashers were at work securing the balks in place.

"Shove off!"

The first was floated to the mooring stakes and a second boat was moved into position.

"Chess!"

Another column of yearlings moved forward, each with a heavy plank on his shoulder. It was heavy, hot, hard and dirty work. Outsiders who imagine that the Military Academy is engaged in turning out "uniformed dudes" should see this work done by the cadets.

Almost with the speed of magic the planks were laid in an orderly manner forming a secure flooring over the balks.

The second boat was anchored, and then a third, a fourth. As the bridge grew Cadet Prescott walked out on the flooring that he might be at the best point for directing the efforts.

As the fifth boat reached its position, Dick turned to see that all was going well.

The yearlings, whose duty it was to carry the balks——"balk-chasers," they were termed unofficially——were standing idle, though alert. They could not move until Mr. Jordan, of the first class, gave the order.

And Jordan? With one hand hanging at his side, the other resting against the small of his back, he stood gazing absently out over the Hudson.

"Mr. Jordan!" called Dick, hastening back over the planking.

"Sir!" answered the surly cadet, facing him.

"Hurry up the balks, if you please, sir."

With a scowl, Jordan turned slowly toward the waiting yearlings.

"Lay hold!" commanded Jordan, and, though it was hard work, the yearlings responded willingly. This was what they were here for, and this hard work was all part of the training that was to fit them for command after they were graduated.

"All possible speed, Mr. Jordan!" admonished Prescott, with a tinge of impatience in his voice.

"Lay hold! Raise! Shoulder!" drawled Mr. Jordan, with tantalizing slowness.

The yearling squad, each man feeling the cut of the sharp corners of the heavy balk on his right shoulder, yet, bearing it patiently, awaited the next command.

"Mr. Jordan, this is not a loafing contest," admonished Prescott in a low voice.

"For——ward!" ordered Jordan with provoking deliberation.

The yearlings under him, made of vastly better material, sprang forward with their balks, laying them in record time across the top of the next pontoon. The lashers then fell upon their work of securing the balks as though they loved labor.

"Chess!" called Dick, remaining on shore this time, and the yearlings with the planks hastened forward, each carrying a plank. Here and there, a lighter cadet staggered somewhat under the plank he was carrying, yet hastened forward to finish his duty of the moment with military speed.

Another pontoon was ready.

"Balks!" called Cadet Prescott. "Balks!"

Jordan got his squad started at last.

Dick glanced swiftly, but in wonder at Lieutenant Armstrong. That Army officer, however, seemed industriously thinking about something else.

"Jordan is truly taking charge of the balks!" muttered Prescott to himself. "He is going to balk me so that I can't get the bridge constructed before recall!"

"Running the balk chasers" is always unpopular work among the cadets. Properly done, this work calls for a great deal of alertness, speed and precision. It is work that takes every moment of the cadet's time and attention, and incessant running in the hot sun. Yet Prescott had, before this, chased the balk carriers, and had not objected. He had taken up that task as he did all others, as part of the day's work, something to be done speedily, well and uncomplainingly.

"What's the matter with you, Mr. Jordan?" asked Dick in an undertone. "Are you sick?"

"Sick of such emigrant's jobs as this!" growled Jordan. "What made you give me———"

"I can't discuss that with you," replied Cadet Dick Prescott coldly. "I shall be compelled to make it an official matter, however, if you hinder me any more."

"Lay hold! Raise! Shoulder! Forward!" Jordan ran with the squad. "Halt! Lower!"

"I reckon Jordan means to keep really on the job now," murmured Prescott to himself, and returned to the advancing end of the pontoon as it crawled over the little arm of the Hudson.

Two more boats, however, and then Dick sprang sternly ashore.

"Mr. Anstey!" called Prescott, and Anstey, the sweet-tempered Virginian, one of Dick's staunchest friends in the corps of cadets, came quickly up, saluting.

"Mr. Anstey, you will chase the balk carriers," directed Dick. "Please try to make up the time that has been lost. Mr. Jordan, you are relieved from your duty, and will report yourself to the instructor for gross lack of promptness in executing orders!"

There could be no mistaking the quality of the justly aroused temper that lay behind Cadet Prescott's flashing blue eyes.

As for Cadet Jordan, that young man's face went instantly livid. He clenched his fists, while the blackness of a storm was on his features.

"Mr. Prescott," he demanded, "do you realize what you are saying———what you are doing?"

"You are relieved. You will report yourself to the instructor, sir!" Dick cut in tersely.

Anstey was already chasing the yearling squad out with the balks, and the young men were moving fast.

As for Dick Prescott, he did not favor Mr. Jordan with a further glance or word, but walked with swift step back to the task of which he was in charge.

With face flushed, Mr. Jordan walked over to the instructor, reporting himself as directed.

"Dismissed from to-day's instruction," said the Army officer briefly. "Wait and return with the detachment, however."

So Cadet Jordan, first class, saluted, turned on his heel, sought the nearest shady spot and sat down to wait.

His body idle, the young man had plenty of time to think——about Cadet Captain Dick Prescott.

"There's nothing to Prescott but swagger and cheap airs," decided Mr. Jordan, idly tossing pebbles. "It's a pity he can't be taken down a peg or two! And now I'm in for demerits before the academic year starts. Probably I shall have to walk punishment tours, too!"

Somehow, Jordan had come along through his more than three years in the corps without attracting much attention.

He had made no strong friends; even Jordan's roommate, Atterbury, felt that he knew the man but slightly.

True, Jordan had not so far been strongly suspected of being morose or surly; he had escaped being ostracized, but he certainly was not popular. If he had made no strong friendships, neither had he so deported himself as to win enmity or even dislike. He was regarded simply as a very taciturn fellow who desired to be let alone, and his apparent wish in this respect was gratified.

Dick Prescott was of an entirely different character. Open, sunny, frank, manly, he was a born leader among men, as he had always been among boys.

Dick was a stickler for duty. He was in training to become an officer of the Regular Army of the United States, and Prescott felt that no man could be a good soldier until the duty habit had become fixed. So, in his earlier years at West Point, Dick had sometimes been unpopular with certain elements among the cadets because he would not greatly depart from what he believed to be his duty as a cadet and a gentleman.

Readers of the *High School Boys' Series* will recall that Prescott, in his home town of Gridley, had been the head of Dick & Co., a sextette of chums and High School athletes. It was in his High School days that young Prescott had developed the qualities of manliness which the Military Academy at West Point was now rounding off for him.

Readers of the preceding volumes in this series, *Dick Prescott's First Year at West Point, Dick Prescott's Second Year at West Point* and *Dick Prescott's Third Year at West Point*, are already familiar with the young man's career as a cadet at the United States Military Academy. Our readers know how hard the fight had been for Dick Prescott, who, in addition to his early struggles to keep his place in scholarship in the corps, had been submitted to the evil work of enemies in the corps. Some of these enemies had been exposed in the end, and forced to leave the Military Academy, but many had been the bitter hours that Prescott had spent under one cloud or another as the result of the wicked work of these enemies.

At last, however, Prescott and his roommate and chum, Greg Holmes, had reached the first class. They had now less than a year to go before they would be graduated and commissioned as officers in the Army.

On reaching first-class dignity, both Dick and Greg had been delighted over their appointment as cadet officers. Prescott was captain of A company and Greg Holmes first lieutenant of the same company.

With Anstey chasing the balk carriers, and all the other squads attending briskly to business, the pontoon was quickly built, so that a roadway extended from shore to shore.

Now came the supreme test as to whether Prescott had done his work well.

In the shade of the nearest trees a team of mules had dozed while the bridge construction was going on. Behind the mules was hitched a loaded wagon belonging to the Engineer Corps.

"Sir," reported Prescott, approaching Lieutenant Armstrong and saluting, "I have the honor to report that the bridge is constructed."

Lieutenant Armstrong returned the salute, next called to an engineer soldier. "Carter!"

"Sir," answered the engineer private, saluting.

"Drive your team over the bridge and back."

Mounting to the seat of his wagon, the soldier obeyed.

Dick Prescott and his mates did not watch this test closely. They were sure enough of the quality of the work that they had done.

Reaching land at the further side of the bridge, the engineer soldier turned his team in a half circle, once more drove upon the bridge and recrossed to the starting point.

"Very well done, Mr. Prescott," nodded the Engineer officer, with a satisfied smile.

"Take down the bridge," ordered Dick, after having saluted the Army instructor.

Working as hard as before, the young men of the third and first classes began to demolish the bridge that they had constructed.

When this had been done, and Dick had officially reported the fact, Lieutenant Armstrong replied:

"Mr. Prescott, you will form your detachment and march back to camp."

"Very good, sir."

Always that same salute with which a man in the Army receives an order.

Some thirty seconds later, the detachment was formed and Dick was marching it back up the inclined road on the way to the summer encampment. By that time, a sergeant and a squad of Engineer privates—soldiers of the Regular Army—were busy taking care of the pontoon boats and other bridge material.

Marching his men inside the encampment, Dick halted them.

"Detachment dismissed!" he called out.

There was a quick break for first and third class tents. These young men were in field uniforms—sombreros, gray flannel shirts, flannel trousers and leggings. Most of them were dripping with perspiration under the hot August sun.

They were all hot and dusty, and their hands stained with tar. Within a very few minutes every man in the detachment must be washed irreproachably clean, without sign of perspiration. They must be in uniforms of immaculate white

7

duck trousers and gray fatigue blouses, wearing cleanly polished shoes, and ready to march to dinner.

A great deal to be accomplished in a few minutes by the average American boy! Yet let one of these cadets be late at dinner formation, without an unquestionably good excuse, and he must pay the penalty in demerits. These demerits, according to their number, bring loss of prized privileges.

Cadet Jordan, having done little, was among the first to be clean and presentable. Immaculate, trim and trig he looked as he stepped from his tent, but on his face lay a scowl that boded ill for his appetite at the coming dinner.

Dick was a master of swift toilets. He was on the company street almost immediately after Jordan had stepped out under the shadow of a tree.

"Prescott," began Jordan stiffly, "I want a word or two with you."

"Yes?" asked Dick, looking keenly at his classmate. "Very good."

"Why did you report me this morning?"

"Because you performed the work in an indolent, laggard manner, even after I had cautioned you."

"Do you consider yourself called upon to be a judge of your classmates?"

"When I am detailed in command over them in any duty—-yes."

"Shall I tell you what I think of you for reporting me?"

"It would be in bad taste, at least," Dick answered. "It is against the regulations for a cadet to call another to account for reporting him officially."

"Oh, bother the regulations!"

"If that is actually your view," replied Dick, with a smile, "then I will leave you to the enjoyment of your discovery concerning the regulations."

"Prescott, you are a prig!" snapped Mr. Jordan.

"If it were necessary to determine that, as a matter of fact," answered Dick coolly, though he flushed somewhat, "I would rather leave it to a decision of the class."

"Oh, I know you have plenty of bootlicks," sneered Jordan. "I also know that you are class president. But that is no reason why you should act as though you thought yourself a bigger man than the President of the United States."

"Jordan, has the sun been affecting your head this forenoon?" demanded Dick, with another keen look at his classmate.

"Well, you do act as though you thought yourself bigger than the President," insisted Jordan sneeringly.

"I am a cadet, not yet capable of being a second lieutenant, in the Army," Dick replied, regaining his coolness. "The President is commander-in-chief of the combined Army and Navy."

"You are utterly puffed up with your own importance," cried Jordan hotly, though in a discreetly low voice. "Prescott, you are———-"

Something in Jordan's eyes warned Dick that a vile insult was coming in an instant.

"*Stop!*" commanded Prescott, shooting a look full of warning at his classmate. "Jordan, don't say anything that will compel me to knock you down in plain sight of the camp. It's years since such a thing as that has happened at West Point!"

8

"Oh, you lordly brute!" sneered Jordan, his face alternately white and aflame with unreasoning anger. "Prescott, you had it in for me. That was why you reported me this morning. That was why you put me in line for demerits and punishment tour walking. You are bound to use your little, petty authority to humble and humiliate me. I shall call you out for this!"

"If you do," shot back Dick, "I shall decline to fight you. It would be against regulations and against all the traditions of the corps for me to arbitrate, by a fight, the question of whether I did right to report you."

"You refuse a fight," warned Jordan, with a malicious grin, "and I'll denounce you all through the class!"

"Denounce me, then, if you wish," retorted Dick in cool contempt, "and you'll bring trouble down on your own head instead. No class requires, or permits, a member to fight in defence of his official conduct."

"Prescott is turning coward, then, is he?"

"You or any other man who presumes to say it knows well enough that he is thereby lying," came quickly from between Prescott's teeth.

"Why, hang you, you———"

"You'd better hush for a moment," warned Prescott. "Here comes the corps adjutant, and I think he is looking for you."

"Yes! With a message of discipline from the O.C. just because I was reported by a toy martinet like you!" retorted Cadet Jordan.

Cadet Filson, corps adjutant, wearing his white gloves, red sash and sword, came up with brisk military stride. He halted before Jordan, while Prescott moved away.

"Mr. Jordan, by order of the commandant of cadets, you will confine yourself to the company street, leaving it only under proper orders. This, for being reported this morning during the tour of engineer instruction. Any further punishment that is to be meted out to you will be published in orders at dress parade this afternoon.

"Very good, sir," replied Cadet Jordan, choking with rage.

Wheeling about, Adjutant Filson strode away again.

The moment he was gone, Jordan, his brow black with fury, stepped over to Prescott.

"So!" he hissed. "The thunderbolt of punishment has fallen, Mr. Prescott. As for you———"

"Mr. Jordan," broke in Dick coolly, "you are ordered to confine yourself to the company street. At this moment you are outside that limit. You will return immediately to the company street!"

Jordan glared, but he had discretion enough left to obey, for Prescott was speaking now as cadet commander of A company, to which company Mr. Jordan belonged.

"Oh, I'll pay you back for this!" raged the disciplined cadet, trembling as he stepped forward.

By this time, many other cadets were out in the company street. Soon after the loud, snappy tones of the bugle summoned the two battalions to dinner formation.

A little while before Cadet Adjutant Filson had approached Jordan, the commandant of cadets, sitting in his tent over by post number one, had sent for the Engineer instructor of the forenoon.

"Mr. Armstrong," asked the commandant, "how much is there in this report against Mr. Jordan this morning? Does Mr. Jordan deserve severe discipline?"

"In my opinion he does, sir," replied Lieutenant Armstrong. "I had the whole happening under observation, though I pretended not to see it."

"Why did you make such pretence, Mr. Armstrong?"

"Because I was watching to see how a man like Mr. Prescott would conduct himself when in command."

Lieutenant Armstrong then related all of the particulars that he had seen of Jordan's conduct.

"Then I am very glad that Mr. Prescott reported Mr. Jordan," replied the commandant of cadets. "Mr. Jordan is a first classman and should be above any such conduct. We will confine Mr. Jordan to his company street for one week; and on Wednesday and Saturday afternoons during the continuance of the encampment, he shall walk punishment tours."

Then the commandant of cadets had passed the word for Cadet Adjutant Filson, to whom he had entrusted the order that the reader has already seen delivered.

But Jordan, unable to realize that he had proved himself unfit as a soldier found his hatred of Dick Prescott growing with every step of the march that carried the cadet corps to dinner at the cadet mess hall.

"Prescott may feel mighty big and proud now!" growled the disgruntled one. "But will he——when I get through with him?"

CHAPTER II

JORDAN REACHES OUT FOR REVENGE

"Hello, there, Stubbs!" called Jordan from the doorway of his tent.

"Oh, that you, Jordan?" called Stubbs.

"Yes; come in, won't you?"

Cadet Stubbs, of the first class, looked slightly surprised, for he had never been an intimate of this particular cadet.

"What's the matter?" asked Stubbs, pushing aside the tent flap and stepping into the tent.

Then, remembering something he had heard, Stubbs continued quickly:

"You're in a little trouble of some kind, aren't you, old man?"

"Oh, I'm in con." growled Mr. Jordan.

"Con." is the brief designation for "confinement."

"Some report this morning, eh?"

"Yes; that dog Prescott sprung a roorback on me. Sit down, won't you?"

"No, thank you," replied Cadet Stubbs more coolly. "Jordan, `dog' is a pretty extreme word to apply to a brother cadet."

"Oh, are you one of that fellow's admirers?" demanded the man in con.

"I've always been an admirer of manliness," replied Stubbs boldly.

"Then how can you stand for a bootlick?" shot out Jordan angrily.

"I don't stand for a bootlick," replied Cadet Stubbs. "I never did."

"Now, I don't want to play baby," went on Jordan half eagerly. "I'm not resenting, on my own account, what happened to-day. But it was an outrage on general principles, for the affair made a fool of me before a lot of new yearlings. Stubbs, we're first classmen, and we shouldn't be humiliated before yearlings in this manner."

"I wasn't there," replied Stubbs. "I was over at the rifle range, you know."

"Then I'll tell you what happened."

Cadet Jordan began a narration of the scene that had ended in his being relieved from engineering instruction that forenoon. Jordan didn't exactly lie, which is always a dangerous thing for a West Point cadet to do, but he colored his narrative so cleverly as to make it rather plain that Cadet Prescott had acted beyond his real authority.

"Still," argued Stubbs doubtfully, "there must have been some reason. I've known Prescott ever since he entered the Academy, and I never saw anything underhanded in him."

"I wouldn't call it underhanded, either," explained Jordan. "Prescott's manner with me might much better be described as overbearing."

"It would have been underhanded, had he reported you when you were really doing nothing unmilitary or improper," interposed Stubbs quickly.

"Are you trying to defend the fellow?" demanded Jordan swiftly.

"No; Prescott, I think, is always quite ready to attend to his own defence. But I'm astonished, Jordan, at the charge you make against him, and I'm trying to understand it."

"What I object to, more than anything else," insisted Jordan, "was his making a fool of me before new yearlings. That is where I think the greatest grievance lies. First classmen are men of some dignity. We are not to be treated like plebes, especially by any members of our own class who may be dressed in a little brief authority. Sit down, won't you, Stubbs?"

"No, thank you, Jordan. I must be on my way soon."

"But I want to get you and a half a dozen other representative first classmen together," wheedled Jordan. "I think we should all talk this over as a strictly class matter. Then, if I'm convinced that I'm in the wrong, I'm going to stop talking."

Crafty Jordan didn't mean exactly what he said.

He would stop talking, if convinced, but he didn't intend to be convinced. He was after Dick Prescott's scalp. Jordan well knew that, at West Point (and at Annapolis, too, for that matter) class action against a man is severer and more irrevocable than even any action that the authorities of the Military Academy itself can take. He wanted to put Prescott wholly in the wrong in the matter. Class action could, at need, drive Prescott out of the corps and end his connection with the Army. For, if a man be condemned by his class at West Point, the feud is carried over into the Army as long as the offender against class ethics dares try to remain in the service.

At the least, Jordan hoped to stir up class feeling to such an extent that, if Prescott were not actually "cut" by class action, at least his popularity would be greatly dimmed.

"So won't you take part in the meeting?" coaxed Jordan, as Cadet Stubbs moved toward the door.

"I don't believe I will," replied Mr. Stubbs. "I'd feel out of place in such a crowd, for I've always considered myself Prescott's friend."

"Do you place your friendship for Prescott above the dignity and honor of the class?" demanded Jordan.

Stubbs flushed.

"I don't believe I'll stay, Jordan, thank you. But I can offer you some advice, if you feel in need of any."

"Yes? Commence firing!"

"Go slow in your grudge against Prescott. Personally, I don't want to see either of you hurt."

"Oh, Prescott won't really be hurt," sneered Jordan. "He told me flatly that he'd decline any calling out that I might attempt."

"You——you didn't try to call him out, did you?"

"I hinted that I might do so."

"Call him out for reporting you?"

"Oh, I didn't specify what the cause of the challenge would be," returned Jordan airily and with a knowing wink.

"Jordan, old fellow, you don't mean that you'd call a cadet out for reporting you officially? Why, that's against every tenet we have. And if such a challenge came to the ears of the superintendent, or of the commandant of cadets, you'd be fired out of the corps before you'd have time to turn around twice."

"Who'd carry the tale that I did call Prescott out?" retorted Cadet Jordan, with a knowing leer.

"Prescott would, if he were a tenth part of the bootlick that you represent him to be," replied Stubbs.

"Better stay, old man; and I'll call in a few others."

"No, sir," returned Cadet Stubbs, with a shake of his head. "The further I go into this matter the less I like it. I'm on my way, Jordan."

Within half an hour, however, Cadet Jordan had found three members of the first class who were willing to listen to him. The matter was threshed out very fully. Jordan, to his listeners, pooh poohed at the idea that he was "sore" on his own account. He posed, and rather well, as the champion of first-class dignity.

"I think you're on the right track, Jordan," assented Durville rather heartily. Durville was one of the few who had never liked Dick well. Durville had always been one of the "wild" ones, and Prescott's ideas of soldierly duty had grated a good deal on Durville's own beliefs.

"The class won't take severe action, anyway," hinted Tupper. "We might vote to give Prescott a week's 'silence,' but any permanent 'cut' would be out of the question. The man has done too many things to make himself popular."

"Besides," chimed in Brown, "look at the place Prescott holds on the Army football eleven. Why he——and Holmes, too, of course——were the pair who saved us from the Navy last November. And we rely upon that pair to a tremendous extent for the successes we expect this coming fall."

Jordan's jaw dropped. In the heat of his anger he had lost sight of the football situation. Prescott and Holmes certainly were the prize players of the Army eleven.

"Well, it might do if the class decided on the 'silence' for Prescott for a week," assented Jordan dubiously.

Then, all of a sudden, he brightened as the thought flashed through his mind:

"If Prescott gets the 'silence,' even for a day, he'll be so furious that he'll do half a dozen fool things that I can provoke him into. Then he'll go so far, in his wrath, that the class will cut him for good and all, and he'll buy his ticket home!"

The more Jordan thought this over, while he pretended to be listening to what his classmates were saying, the surer the cadet plotter felt that he could work his enemy out of the corps within the next week or so.

"Well, I dare say that you fellows are right in advising milder measures," admitted Jordan at last. "Of course, though I try not to let my personal feelings enter into this at all, yet I suppose I can't keep my sense of outraged class dignity wholly untainted by my personal feelings. Besides, the 'silence' for a week will doubtless cover all the needs of the case, and I don't bear the fellow any personal grudge, or I try not to."

"That's a sensible, manly view, Jordan," chimed in Brown, "and it does you credit as a gentleman and a man of honor. Now, you know, it's a fearful thing for a man who has reached the first class to have to drop his Army career at the last moment. So we'll try to bring the majority of the class around to the idea of the week's 'silence.'"

"Now, lest it appear as though I were actuated by personal motives," continued Jordan, "I'll have to stand back and let you fellows do the talking with the other men of the class."

"That's all right," nodded Durville. "We wholly understand the delicacy of your position, and we can attend to it all right. Besides, all we have to do, anyway, is to ascertain how the class feels on the matter."

"Don't let it be lost sight of, though," begged Jordan, almost betraying his over anxiety, "that it is a serious matter of class dignity and honor."

"We won't, old man," promised Durville, as the visitors rose.

As soon as he was alone——for his tentmate was away on a cavalry drill, Jordan rose, his eyes flashing with triumph.

"Dick Prescott, I believe I have you where I want you! What a rage you'll be in, if you get the 'silence'! 'Whom the gods would destroy they first make mad,'" Jordan went on, under his breath, wholly unaware that he had parodied the meaning of that famous quotation. "You'll rage with anger, Prescott. You'll do the very things that will warrant the class in giving you the long 'cut.'"

The "silence" is a form of rebuke that the cadet corps, once in many years, administers to one of the many Army officers who are stationed over them. When the cadet corps decides to give an officer the "silence," the proceeding is a unique one.

Whenever an officer under this ban approaches a group of cadets they cease talking, and remain silent as long as he is near them. They salute the officer; they make any official communications that may be required, and do so in a faultlessly respectful manner; they answer any questions addressed to them by the officer under ban. But they will not talk, while he is within hearing, on anything except matters of duty.

An officer under the ban of the "silence" may approach a gathering of a hundred or more cadets, all talking animatedly until they perceive his approach. Then, all in an instant, they become mute. The officer may remain in their neighborhood for an hour, yet, save upon an official matter, no cadet will speak until the officer has moved on.

This "silence" may be given an officer for a stated number of days, or it may be made permanent. It has sometimes happened that an officer has been forced to ask a transfer from West Point to some other Army station, simply because he could not endure the "silence."

Very rarely, indeed, the silence is given to a cadet; it is more especially applicable if he be a cadet officer who is in the habit of reporting his fellow classmen for what they may consider insufficient breaches of discipline.

The "cut" or "Coventry" is reserved for the cadet whom it is intended to drive from the Army altogether. If a man at West Point is "sent to Coventry" by the whole corps, or as a result of class action, he will never be able to form friendships in the Army again, no matter how long he remains in the Army, or how hard he tries to fight the sentence down.

Cadet Jordan, as will have been noted, professed to be satisfied if the class voted a week's "silence" to Dick Prescott, for Jordan believed that by this time the tantalized young cadet captain could be provoked into actions that would bring the imposition of the "long silence" of permanent Coventry.

At the end of the busy cadet day, when the two cadet battalions stood in formal array at dress parade, Cadet Adjutant Filson published the day's orders.

One of these orders mentioned Jordan's confinement to the company street, and added the further infliction of "punishment tours" to be walked every Wednesday and Saturday afternoons.

"Oh, well," thought the culprit, savagely, "as I walk I can plan newer and newer things. I'll go into the Army, and you, Prescott, may become a freight clerk on a jerk-water railroad."

Unknown to either Jordan or Prescott at that moment, other storm-clouds were gathering swiftly over the head of the popular young cadet captain.

CHAPTER III

CATCHING A MAN FOR BREACH OF "CON."

Lieutenant Denton was the tac. who served as O.C. during this tour of twenty-four hours.

A "tac.," as has been explained in earlier volumes, is a Regular Army officer who is on duty in the department of tactics. All of the tacs. are subordinates of the commandant of cadets, the latter officer being in charge of the discipline and tactical training of cadets. Each tac. is, in turn, for a period of twenty-four hours, officer in charge, or "O.C."

During the summer encampment of the cadets, the O.C. occupies a tent at headquarters, and is in command, under the commandant, of the camp.

14

It was in the evening, immediately after the return of the corps from supper, when Lieutenant Denton had sent for Cadet Captain Prescott.

"Mr. Prescott," began the O.C., "there has been some trouble, lately, as you undoubtedly know, with plebes running the guard after taps. Now, our plebes are men very new to the West Point discipline, and they do not appreciate the seriousness of their conduct. Until the young men have had a little more training, we wish, if possible, to save them from the consequences of their lighter misdeeds. Of course, if a cadet, plebe or otherwise, is actually found outside the guard line after taps, then we cannot excuse his conduct. This is where the ounce of prevention comes in. Mr. Prescott, I wish you would be up and around the camp between taps and midnight to-night. Keep yourself in the background a bit, and see if you can stop any plebes who may be prowling before they have had a chance to get outside the guard lines. If you intercept any plebes while they are still within camp limits, demand of them their reasons for being out of their tents. If the reasons are not entirely satisfactory, turn them over to the cadet officer of the day. Any plebe so stopped and turned over to the cadet officer of the day will be disciplined, of course, but his punishment will be much lighter than if he were actually caught outside the guard lines. You understand your instructions, Mr. Prescott?"

"Perfectly, sir."

"That is all, Mr. Prescott."

Saluting, Dick turned and left the tent.

"That's just like Lieutenant Denton," thought Dick, as he marched away to his own company street. "Some of the tacs. would just as soon see the plebe caught cold, poor little beast. But Lieutenant Denton can remember the time when he was a cadet here himself, and he wants to see the plebe have as much of the beginner's chance as can be given."

As Dick pushed aside the flap and entered his tent, he beheld his chum and roommate, Greg Holmes, now a cadet lieutenant, carefully transferring himself to his spoony dress uniform.

"Going to the hop to-night, old ramrod?" asked Greg carelessly, though affectionately.

"Not in my line of hike," yawned Prescott. "You know I'm no hopoid."

"Oh, loyal swain!" laughed Greg in mock admiration. "You hop but little oftener than once a year, when Laura comes on from the home town! You throw away nearly all of the pleasures of the waxed floor."

"Even though but once a year, I go as often as I want," Dick answered, with a pleasant smile.

"But see here, ramrod, an officer is expected to be a gentleman, and a fellow can't be an all-around gentleman unless he is at ease with the ladies. What sort of practice do you give yourself?"

"You're dragging a femme to the hop tonight?" queried Dick.

"Yes, sir," admitted Greg promptly.

"Then you're——pardon me——you're engaged to the young lady, of course?"

"Engaged to take her to the hop, of course," parried Holmes.

"And engaged to be married to her, as well," insisted Dick.

"Ye-es," admitted Cadet Holmes reluctantly. "Let me see; this is the fourteenth girl you've been engaged to marry, isn't it?"

"No, sir," blurted Greg indignantly. "Miss——I mean my present betrothed, is only the eighth who has done me the honor."

"Even eight fiancees is going it pretty swiftly for a cadet not yet through West Point," chuckled Dick.

"Well, confound it, it isn't my fault, is it?" grumbled Greg. "I didn't break any of the engagements. The other seven girls broke off with me. On the whole, though, I'm rather obliged to the seven for handing me the mitten, for I'm satisfied that Miss——I mean, the present young lady——is the one who is really fitted to make me happy for life."

"I'm almost sorry I'm not going to-night," mused Prescott aloud. "Then I'd see the fortunate young lady."

"Oh, there are no secrets from you, old ramrod," protested Greg good-humoredly. "You know her, anyway, I think——Miss Steele."

"Captain Steele's daughter?"

"Precisely," nodded Greg.

"Daughter of one of the instructors in drawing?"

"Yes."

"Greg, you're at least practical this time," laughed Dick. "That is, you will be if Miss Steele doesn't follow the example of her predecessors, and break the engagement too soon."

"Practical?" repeated Cadet Holmes. "What are you talking about, old ramrod? Has the heat been too much for you to-day? Practical! Now, what on earth is there that's practical about a love affair?"

"Why, if this engagement lasts long enough, Greg, old fellow, Captain Steele and his wife will simply have to send you an invitation to a Saturday evening dinner at their quarters. And then, in ordinary good nature, they'll have to invite me, also, as your roommate. Greg, do you stop to realize that we've never yet been invited to an officer's house to dinner?"

"And we never would be, if we depended on you," grumbled Greg. "Women are the foundation rock of society, yet you never look at anyone in a petticoat except Laura Bentley, who comes here only once a year, and who may be so tired of coming here that she'll never appear again."

A brief cloud flitted across Dick's face. Seeing it, repentant Greg rattled on:

"Of course you know me well enough, old ramrod, to know that I'm not really reproaching you for being so loyal to Laura, good, sweet girl that she is. But you've miffed a lot, of the girls on the post by your constancy. Why, you could have the younger daughters of a dozen officers' following you, if you'd only look at them."

"The younger daughters of the officers are all in the care of nurse-maids, Greg," Prescott retorted with pretended dignity. "Relieving nurse-maids of their responsibilities is no part of a cadet's training or duty."

16

"Well, 'be good and you'll be happy'——but you won't have a good time," laughed Greg, who, having finished his inspection of himself in the tiny glass, was now ready to depart.

"On your way, Holmesy," nodded Dick, glancing at the time. "It's a long walk, even for a cadet, to Captain Steele's quarters."

Greg went away, humming under his breath.

"There's a chap whom care rarely hits," mused Dick, looking half enviously after his chum. "I wonder really if he ever will marry?"

Presently Dick picked up his camp chair and placed it just outside at the door of his tent. It was pleasant to sit there in the semi-gloom.

But presently he began to wonder, a little, that none of the fellows dropped around for a chat, for he was aware that a number of the first classmen were not booked for the hop that night.

From time to time Dick saw a first classman enter or leave the tent of Cadet Jordan.

"He seems unusually popular to-night," thought Prescott, with a smile. "Well, better late than never. Poor Jordan has never been much of a favorite before. I wonder if my reporting him to-day has made the fellows take more notice of him? It is a rare thing, these days, for a first classman to be confined to his company street."

For Prescott the evening became, in fact, so lonely that presently he rose, left the encampment and strolled along the road leading to the West Point Hotel. On other than hop nights, this road was likely to be crowded with couples. That night, however, nearly all of the young ladies at West Point had been favored with invitations to Cullum Hall.

Tattoo was sounding just as Prescott crossed the line at post number one on reentering camp. In half an hour more, it would be taps. At taps, all lights in tents were expected to be out, and the cadets, save those actually on duty, to be in their beds. An exception was made in favor of cadets who had received permission to escort young ladies to the hop. Each cadet who had to return to the hotel, or to officers' quarters with a young lady had received the needed permission, and the time it would take him to go to the young lady's destination and return to camp was listed at the guard tent. Any cadet who took more than the permitted time to escort his partner of the hop to her abiding place would be subject for report.

However, the special duty imposed upon Cadet Prescott for this night related to plebes, and plebes do not go to the hops.

Bringing out his camp chair, Dick sat once more before his tent. Down at Jordan's tent he could still hear the low hum of cadet voices.

"Something is certainly going on there," mused Prescott.

For a moment or two he felt highly curious; then he repressed that feeling.

"Good evening, Prescott."

"Oh, good evening, Stubbs."

Cadet Stubbs came to a brief halt before the cadet captain's tent.

"I have been noticing that Jordan has a good many visitors this evening," Dick remarked.

17

"All from our class, too, aren't they?" questioned Stubbs.

"Yes. If we were yearlings I should feel sure that they had a plebe or two in there. But first classmen don't haze plebes."

"No; we don't haze plebes," replied Cadet Stubbs with a half sigh, for Prescott was the only first classman at present in camp who did not fully know just what was in progress at Jordan's tent.

But West Point men pride themselves on bearing no tales, so Stubbs repressed the longing to explain to Dick what Jordan was seeking to bring about.

As a matter of fact, though some of the members of the first class were hot-headed enough to accept Jordan's view of the report against him, the class sentiment was considerably against the motion to give Cadet Captain Richard Prescott the silence, even for a week.

However, none came near Prescott to talk it over. That again would be tale-bearing. Dick was not likely to hear of the move unless summoned to present his own defense in the face of class charges.

Nor would Greg be approached on the subject. The accused man's roommate or tentmate is always left out of the discussion.

Taps sounded; almost immediately the lights in the tents went out. Stillness settled over the encampment.

The fact that a single candle remained lighted in Prescott's tent showed that he had permission to run a light. The assumption would be that he was engaged on some official duty, though the fact of running a light did not in any way betray the nature of that duty.

Dick sat inside at first. Then, one by one, the cadets returning from the hop stepped through the company streets. At last Greg Holmes came in.

"Still engaged, Holmesy?" asked Dick, looking up with a quizzical smile.

"Surest thing on the post!" returned Greg, with a radiant smile. He had the look of being a young man very much in love and utterly happy over his good fortune.

"Going to run a light?" asked Holmes, gaping, as he swiftly disrobed.

"Yes; but I'll throw the tin can around so that the blaze won't be in your eyes."

"It won't anyway," retorted Greg, turning down the cover of his bed. "I'll turn my back on the glim."

The "tin can" is a device time-honored among cadets in the summer encampment. It is merely a reflector, made of an old tin can, that increases and concentrates the brilliancy of the candle light. The "tin can" may also be used in such a way as to throw a large part of a tent in semi-darkness.

Two minutes later, Greg's breathing proclaimed the fact that this cadet was sound asleep.

Dick, stifling a yawn——for it had been a long, hard and busy day——threw a look of envy toward his chum. Then, in uniform, Prescott stepped out into the company street.

It was a dark, starless night; an ideal night to a plebe who wanted to run the guard and put in some time outside of the camp limits.

Keeping as much in the shadow as he could, Prescott stepped along until he came near one of the sentry lines.

For some time he stood thus, eyes and ears alert, though he lounged in the shadow where he was not likely to be seen.

"It's an off night for plebe mischief, I reckon," he murmured at last. "All the plebes are good little boys to-night, and safely tucked in their cribs."

At last, when it was near midnight, Prescott came out from his place of semi-concealment and stepped over near the guard line.

It was not long ere a yearling sentry, with bayonet fixed and gun resting over his right shoulder, came pacing toward the first classman.

Recognizing a cadet officer, the yearling sentry halted, holding his piece at "present arms."

"Walk your post," Dick directed, after having returned the salute.

Had Prescott been a cadet private the sentry would have questioned him as to his reasons for being out after taps. But with a cadet captain it was different. Though Prescott was not cadet officer of the day, he was privileged to have official reasons for being out without making an accounting to the sentry.

Slowly the yearling sentry paced down to the further end of his post. Then he came back again. Having saluted Prescott recently, he did not pause now, but kept on past the cadet officer standing there in the shadow.

As the sentry's footsteps again sounded softer in the distance, Prescott suddenly became aware of something not far away from him.

It was a little glow of fire, at an elevation of something less than six feet from the ground, over beside a bush.

This glow of fire looked exactly as though it came from a lighted cigar.

If the cigar were held by a civilian, it was a matter that needed looking into.

Cadets, if they wish, may smoke at certain times and within certain limits. But nothing in the regulations permits a cadet to go outside the guard lines after taps to smoke.

Dick Prescott drew further back into the shadow, noiselessly, and kept his eye on the distant glow until he heard the yearling returning.

"Sentry!" called Prescott sharply. The yearling, his piece at port arms, came on the run.

"Investigate that glow yonder," ordered Prescott.

"Very good, sir!"

Prescott and the sentry started together. For an instant the glow wavered, as though the man that was behind the glow meditated taking to his heels.

"Halt!" called the sentry. "Who's there?"

Now the glow disappeared, but cadet captain and sentry were close enough to see the outlines of a figure in cadet uniform.

The figure still moved uncertainly, as though bent on flight.

But the sight of two pursuers seemed to change the unknown's mind.

"A cadet," he called, in answer to the sentry's challenge.

The sentry halted.

"Advance, cadet, to be recognized," he commanded.

Prescott came to a halt not far from the sentry.

Slowly, with evident reluctance, the figure moved forward.

"Mr. Jordan!" called Prescott, in considerable amazement.

19

"Yes, sir," admitted Jordan huskily.

Now, Dick had every reason in the world for not wanting to report this cadet again, but duty is and must be duty, in the Army.

"Mr. Jordan, you are under orders of confinement to the company street," cried Dick sternly.

"Yes, sir."

"And yet you are found outside of camp limits? Have you any explanation to offer, sir?"

"I was nervous, sir," replied Jordan, "and couldn't sleep. So I slipped out past the guard line to enjoy a quieting smoke."

"Smoking causes vastly more nervousness than it ever remedies, Mr. Jordan," replied the young cadet captain. "Have you any additional explanation or excuse for being outside the company street?"

"No, sir."

"Then return to your tent, sir."

"I——I suppose you are going to report this, Mr. Prescott?" asked the other first classman.

"I have no alternative," Dick answered. "You are under confinement to the company street; you have made a breach of confinement, and I am your company commander."

"Very good, sir."

Jordan stiffened up, saluted, then passed on across the guard line, making for the street of A company.

Dick turned back, more slowly, a thoughtful frown gathering on his fine face, while the yearling sentry was muttering to himself:

"Great Caesar, but Prescott surely has put both feet in it. He reports a fellow classman for a little thing like a late smoke, and the man reported will be doomed to go into close arrest! Glad I'm not Prescott!"

It would be untruthful to deny that Dick Prescott was worried; nevertheless, he made his way briskly to the tent of the O.C.

"Jove, what luck!" chuckled Jordan tremulously, as he hastened along the street of A company to his tent. "Of course I'll be in for all sorts of penalties, and I'll have to be mighty good, after this, to keep within safe limits on demerits. But I have Prescott just where I want the insolent puppy! The class, this evening, was much in doubt about giving him the silence. But flow! When he has gone out of his way to catch me in such an innocent little breach of con.! Whew! But my lucky star is surely at the top of the sky to-night."

Cadet Jordan was soon tucked in under his bed cover. He had not fallen asleep, however, when he heard a step coming down the street.

Dick had chanced to find the O.C. still up. In a few words Prescott made his report.

"This is a very serious report against a first classman, Mr. Prescott," said kind-hearted Lieutenant Denton gravely. "It is most unfortunate for Mr. Jordan that he has not a better excuse. You will go to Mr. Jordan's tent, Mr. Prescott, and direct him to remain in his tent, in close arrest, until he hears as to the further disposition of his case by the commandant of cadets."

"Very good, sir," Prescott answered, saluting.

"And then you may go to your own tent and retire, Mr. Prescott. I fancy the plebes have been good to-night."

"Thank you, sir."

With a rather heavy heart, though outwardly betraying no sign, Prescott walked along until he reached Jordan's tent, where he delivered the order from the O.C.

"Did you hear that, old man?" growled Jordan to his tentmate, after the cadet captain had gone.

"Pretty rough!" returned the tentmate sleepily.

Rough? The first class was seething when it received the word next morning, for it was the common belief that Prescott must have shadowed and followed his classmate in order to entrap him.

"It's surely time for class action now," Durville told several of his classmates.

CHAPTER IV

THE CLASS COMMITTEE CALLS

Outwardly A company and the entire corps of cadets was as placid and unruffled as ever when the two battalions marched to breakfast that morning.

One conversant with military procedure, however, would have noted that Jordan, being a prisoner, marched in the line of the file closers.

And Mr. Jordan's face was wholly sulky, strive as he would to banish the look and appear indifferent.

Even to a fellow naturally as unsocial as the cadet now in arrest, it was no joke to be confined to his tent even for the space of a week, except when engaged in official duties; and to be obliged, two afternoons in a week, to march in full equipment and carry his piece, for three hours in the barracks quadrangle under the watchful eyes of a cadet corporal.

This penalty would last during the remaining weeks of the encampment and would be pronounced upon Jordan as soon as the commandant of cadets perfunctorily confirmed the temporary order of Lieutenant Denton.

Dick, at the head of A company, looked as impassive as ever, though he felt far from comfortable.

Through the ranks, wherever first classmen walked, excitement was seething.

When Prescott was seated at table in the cadet mess hall, Greg, who sat next his chum, turned and raised his eyebrows briefly, as though to say:

"There's something warm in the air."

Dick's momentary glance in return as much as said:

"I know it."

None of the other cadets at the same table turned to address Prescott directly, with the single exception of Greg Holmes. True, when Dick had occasion, twice or thrice, to address other men at his table, they answered him, though briefly.

Whatever was in the air it had not broken yet. That was as much as Prescott could guess.

The instant that they had returned to camp, and the two chums were in their tent, Greg whispered fiercely:

"That sulker, Jordan, is putting up trouble for you, as sure as you're alive."

"Then I've given him a bully handle to his weapon," admitted Dick Prescott dryly.

They were hustling into khaki field uniform now, and there was little time for comment; none for Greg to go outside and find out what was really in the air. Battery drill was right ahead of them. Barely were the chums changed to khaki field uniform before the call sounded on the bugle.

On the recall from battery drill, the chums had but a few moments before they were called out for a drill in security and information.

So the time passed until dinner. Again Jordan marched in the line of the file closers, and now this first classman had received his official sentence from the commandant of cadets.

So far as the demeanor of the class toward Prescott was concerned, dinner was an exact repetition of breakfast.

On the return of the corps to camp, a few minutes followed that were officially assigned to recreation.

Dick stood just inside the door of his tent when he heard the tread of several men approaching.

Looking out, he saw seven men of his own class coming up. Durville was at their head.

"Good afternoon, Prescott," began Durville.

"Good afternoon, gentlemen," nodded Dick.

"We represent the class in a little matter," continued Durville, "and I have been asked to be the spokesman. Can you spare us a little time?"

"All the time that I have before the call sounds for my next drill," replied Prescott.

"Mr. Prescott, you reported a member of our class last night," began Durville.

"I did so officially," Dick answered.

"Of course, Mr. Prescott, we understand that. The offender was a member of A company, and you are the cadet captain of that company. But this affair happened at the guard line, and you were not cadet officer of the day. Mr. Jordan feels that you exerted yourself to catch him in his delinquency."

"I did not," replied Prescott promptly. "At the time when I called upon the cadet sentry to apprehend Mr. Jordan, I had not the remotest idea that it was Mr. Jordan."

"Then," asked Durville bluntly, "how did you, who were not the cadet officer of the day, happen to be where you could catch Mr. Jordan so neatly?"

"In that matter I have no explanation to offer," Prescott replied.

One less a stickler for duty than Prescott might have replied that he had been on the spot the night before in obedience to a special order from the officer in charge.

Dick Prescott, however, felt that to make such a statement would be a breach of military faith. The order that he had received from Lieutenant Denton he looked upon as a confidential military order that could not be discussed, except on permission or order from competent military sources.

"Now, Prescott," continued Cadet Durville almost coaxingly, "we don't want to be hard on you, and we don't want to do anything under a misapprehension. Can't you be more explicit?"

"I have already regretted my inability to go further into the matter with you," Dick replied, pleasantly though firmly.

"And you can give us no explanation whatever of how you came to report Jordan for being beyond the camp limits?"

"All I am able to tell you is that my reporting of Mr. Jordan was a regrettable but military necessity."

"Is that all we wish to ask, gentlemen?" inquired Durville, turning to his six companions.

"It ought to be," retorted Brown dryly.

The seven nodded very coldly. Durville turned on his heel, leading the others away.

"Unless I'm a poor kitchen judge, old ramrod, your goose is cooked," muttered Greg Holmes mournfully.

"Then it will have to be," spoke Dick resolutely.

"But you haven't told even me how you came to be, last night, just where you could fall afoul of Jordan so nicely."

"Old chum," cried Dick, turning and resting a hand on Greg's right arm, "I can discuss that matter no further with you than I did with the class committee."

"You're a queer old extremist, anyway, with all your notions of duty and other bugaboos. This affair has given me the shivers."

"Then cheer up, Holmesy!" laughed Cadet Captain Prescott.

"Oh, it's you I'm shivering for," muttered Greg.

CHAPTER V

THE CADET "SILENCE" FALLS

Six companies of sun-browned, muscular young men marched away to cadet mess hall that evening.

If any of these cadets were more than properly fatigued, none of them betrayed the fact. Their carriage was erect, their step springy and martial. In ranks their faces were impassive, but when they filed into the mess hall, seated themselves at table and glanced about, an orderly Babel broke loose.

At all, that is to say, save one table. That was the table at which Cadet Captain Richard Prescott sat.

Greg was the first to make the discovery. He turned to Brown with a remark. Brown glanced at Holmes, nodding slightly. All the other cadets at that board were eating, their eyes on their plates.

"What's the matter?" quizzed Holmes. "You're ideas moving slowly?"

Again Brown glanced up at his questioner, but that was all.

"How's the cold lamb, Durville?" questioned Dick.

Durville passed the meat without speaking, nor did he look directly at Prescott.

Dick and Greg exchanged swift glances. They understood. The blow had fallen.

The Silence had been given!

23

Dick felt a hot flush mounting to his temples. The blood there seemed to sting him. Then, as suddenly, he went white, clammy perspiration beading his forehead and temples.

This was the verdict of the class——of the corps? He had offended the strict traditions and inner regulations of the cadet corps, and was pronounced unfit for association!

That explained the constrained atmosphere at this one table, the one spot in all the big room where silence replaced the merry chatter of mealtime.

"The fellows are mighty unjust!" thought Dick bitterly, as he went on eating mechanically. He no longer knew, really, whether he were eating meat, bread or potato.

That was the first thought of Prescott. But swiftly his view changed. He realized about him, were hundreds of the flower of the young manhood of the United States. These young men were being trained in the ways of justice and honor, and were trying to live up to their ideals.

If such an exceptional, picked body of young men had condemned him——had sentenced him to bitter retribution——was it not wholly likely that there was much justice on their side?

"The verdict of so many good and true men must contain much justice," Prescott thought, as he munched mechanically, trying proudly to bide his dismay from watchful eyes. "Then I have offended against manhood, in some way. Yet how? I have obeyed orders and have performed my duties like a soldier. How, then, have I done wrong?"

Once more it seemed indisputable to Prescott that his comrades had wronged him. But once more his own sense of justice triumphed.

"I am not really at fault," he told himself, "nor is the class. The class has acted on the best view of appearances that it could obtain. I was wholly right in obeying the orders that I received from Lieutenant Denton, and equally right in not communicating those orders to a class committee. Nor could I refrain from reporting Mr. Jordan for breach of con. That was my plain duty, more especially as Mr. Jordan is a member of the company that I command. But the appearances have been all against me, and I have refused to explain. The class is hardly to be blamed for condemning me, and I imagine that Mr. Jordan, in accusing me, has not been at all reticent. Probably, too, he has taken no extreme pains to adhere to the exact truth. I do not see how I can get out of the scrape in which I find myself. I wonder if the silence is to be continued until I am forced to resign and give up a career in the Army?"

With such thoughts as these it was hard, indeed, to look and act as though nothing had happened.

But Cadet Jordan, taking eager, covert looks at his enemy from another table, got little satisfaction from anything that he detected in Prescott's face.

"Why, that b.j.(fresh) puppy is quite equal to cheeking his way on through the last year and into the Army!" thought Jordan maliciously. "However, he's done for! No matter if he sticks, he'll never get any joy out of his shoulder straps."

Little could Jordan imagine that Prescott's proud nature would long resist the silence. If this rebuke were to become permanent, then Prescott was not in the least likely to attempt to enter upon his studies at the beginning of they Academic year in September.

And Greg! He didn't waste any time in trying to be just to any one. All his hot blood rose and fomented within him at the bare thought of this terrible indignity put upon that prince of good fellows, Dick Prescott. Holmes felt, in truth, as though he would be glad to fight, in turn, every member of the first class who had voted for the silence.

That practically all the fellows of the first class had voted for the silence, Greg did not for an instant believe. He was well aware that Dick had many staunch friends in the class who would stand out for him in the face of any appearances. But a vote of the majority in favor of the silence would be enough; the rest of the class would be bound by the action of the majority. And all the lower classes would observe and respect any decision of the first class concerning one of its own members.

Not a word did Greg say to Dick. Yet, under the table, Holmes employed one of his knees to give Dick's knee a long, firm pressure that conveyed the hidden message of unfaltering friendship and loyalty.

For the other cadets at the table the silence imposed more or less hardship, since they could utter only the most necessary words. They however, were not objects against whom the silence was directed, and they could endure the absence of conversation with far more indifference than was possible for Prescott.

It was a relief to all at the table, none the less, when the rising order was given. When the corps had marched back to camp, and had been dismissed, Dick Prescott, head erect, and betraying no sign of annoyance, walked naturally into A company's Street, drew out his camp chair and seated himself on it in the open.

Barely had he done so, when Greg arrived. Cadet Holmes, however, did not stop or speak, but hurried on.

"Greg has his hands full," thought Dick. "He's going to investigate. And I'm afraid his hot head will get him into some sort of trouble, too."

The imposition of the silence did not affect Greg in his relations with his tentmate. When a cadet is sent to Coventry, or has the silence "put" on him, his tentmate or roommate may still talk unreservedly with him without fear of incurring class disfavor. To impose the rule of silence on the tentmate or roommate of the rebuked one would be to punish an innocent man along with the guilty one.

Rarely, after all, does the corps err in its judgment when Coventry or the silence is meted out. None the less, in Dick's case a grave mistake had been made.

Time slipped by, and darkness came on, but Greg had not returned.

There was band concert in camp that night. Many cadets of the first and third classes had already gone to meet girls whom they would escort in strolling near the bandstand. Plebes are not expected to escort young ladies to these concerts. The members of the second class were away on the summer furlough, as Dick and Greg had been the summer before.

As the musicians began to tune up at the bandstand, most of the remaining cadets sauntered through the company streets on their way to get close to the music.

All cadets who passed through A company's street became suddenly silent when within ten paces of Dick's tent, and remained silent until ten paces beyond.

Dick's tent being at the head of the street, he was quite near enough to the music. But he was not long in noting that both cadet escorts and cadets without young ladies took pains not to approach too close to where he sat. It was enough to fill him with savage bitterness, though he still strove to be just to his classmates who had been blinded by Cadet Jordan's villainous scheme.

Of a sudden the band struck up its lively opening march. Just at that moment Prescott became aware of the fact that Greg Holmes was lifting out a campstool and was placing it beside him.

"Well," announced Greg, "I've found out all there is behind the silence."

"I took it for granted that was your purpose," Dick responded.

"Aren't you anxious to hear the news, old ramrod?"

"Yes; very."

"I'm hanged if you look anxious!" muttered Greg, studying his chum's face keenly.

"I fancy I've got to display a good deal of skill in masking my feelings," smiled Dick wearily.

"Oh, I don't know," returned Cadet Holmes hopefully. "It may not turn out to be so bad."

"Then a permanent silence hasn't been imposed?"

"Not yet," replied Greg.

"By which, I suppose, you mean that the length of the silence has not yet been decided upon."

"It hasn't," Greg declared. "It was only after the biggest, swiftest and hardest kind of campaign, in fact, that the class was swung around to the silence. Only a bare majority were wheedled into voting for it. Nearly half of the class stood out for you stubbornly, pointing to your record here as a sufficient answer. And that nearly half are still your warm adherents."

"Yet, of course, they are bound by the majority action?"

"Of course," sighed Greg. "That's the old rule here, isn't it? Well, to sum it up quickly, old ramrod, the silence has been put on you, and that's as far as the decision runs up to date. The class is yet to decide on whether the silence is to be for a week or a month. Of course, a certain element will do all in its power to make the silence a permanent thing. Even if it is made permanent, Dick, you'll stick, won't you?"

"No."

"What?"

"I shall not even try to stick against any permanent silence," replied Prescott slowly.

"I thought you had more fight in you than that," muttered Greg in a tone of astonishment.

"I think I have enough fight," Dick replied with some warmth. "And I honestly believe I have enough in me to make at least a moderately capable officer of the Army. But, Greg, I'm not going to make a stubborn, senseless effort, all through life, to stay among comrades who don't want me, and who will make it plain enough that they do not consider me fit to be of their number. Greg, in such an atmosphere I couldn't bring out the best that is in me. I couldn't make the most of my own life, or do the best by those who are dear to me."

There was an almost imperceptible catch in Dick Prescott's voice. He was thinking of Laura Bentley as the one for whom he had hoped to do all his best things in life.

"I don't know but you're right, old fellow. But it's fearfully hard to decide such a matter off-hand," returned Greg. His own voice broke. For some moments Holmes sat in moody silence.

At last he reached out a hand, resting it on Dick's arm.

"If you get out, old ramrod, it's the outs for me on the same day."

"Greg!"

"Oh, that's all right," retorted Cadet Holmes, trying to force a cheery ring into his voice. "If you can't get through and live under the colors, Dick, I don't want to!"

"But Greg, old fellow, you mustn't look at it that way. You have had three years of training here at the nation's expense. It will soon be four. You owe your country some return for this magnificent training."

"How about you, then?" asked Holmes, regarding his friend quizzically.

"Me? I'd stay under the colors, and give up my life for the country and the Army, if my comrades would have it. But if they won't, then it's for the best interests of the service that I get out, Greg."

"Well, talk yourself blind, if it will give you any relief. But post this information up on your inside bulletin board: When you quit the service, old ramrod, it will be 'good-bye' for little Holmesy!"

CHAPTER VI

TRYING TO EXPLAIN TO THE GIRLS

Breakfast, the next morning, was a repetition of what had happened the night before.

At Dick's table the silence was absolute.

Even Captain Reid, cadet commissary, noticed it and understood, in his trip of inspection through mess hall.

The thing that Reid, who was an Army officer, did not know was——who was the victim? He never guessed Prescott, who was class president, and believed to be one of the tallest of the class idols.

It speaks volumes for the intended justice of the cadets when they will, in time of fancied need, destroy even their idols.

Thus it went on for some days.

Dick performed all of his duties as usual, and as well as usual. Nothing in his demeanor showed how keenly he felt the humiliation that had been put upon him. Only in his failure to attempt any social address of a classmate did he betray his recognition of the silence.

Greg did his best to cheer up his chum. Anstey expressed greatest sorrow and sympathy for his friend Prescott. Holmes promptly reported this conversation to Dick. Other good friends expressed their sorrow to Holmes. In every case he bore the name and the implied message hastily to the young cadet captain.

A few whom Dick had considered his good friends did not thus put themselves on record. Dick thereupon understood that they had acted upon their best information and convictions, and he honored them for being able to put friendship aside in the interests of tradition and corps honor.

The silence had lasted five days when, one evening, a class meeting was called. Though Cadet Prescott was class president, he did not attend, for he knew very well that he was not wanted.

Greg's sense of delicacy told the latter that it was not for him to attend the meeting, either.

The vice president of the class was called to the chair. Then Durville and others made heated addresses in which they declared that Prescott could no longer consistently retain the class presidency.

A motion was made that Prescott be called upon to resign. It was seconded by several first classmen.

Then Anstey, the Virginian, claimed the floor in behalf of the humiliated class president. The blood of Virginian orators flowed in Anstey's veins, nor did he discredit his ancestry.

In an impassioned yet deliberate and logical speech Anstey declared that great injustice had been done Cadet Richard Prescott, and by the members of his own class.

"Every man within reach of my voice knows Mr. Prescott's record," declared the Virginian warmly. "When we were plebes, who stood up most staunchly as our class champion? Why, suh, why did we choose Mr. Prescott as our class president? Was it not because we believed, with all our hearts, that in Richard Prescott lay all the best elements of noble, upright and manly cadethood? Do you remember, suh, and fellow classmen, the wild enthusiasm that prevailed when we, by our suffrages, had declared Mr. Prescott to be our ideal of the man to lead the class in all the paths of honor?"

Anstey paused for an instant. Then, lowering his voice somewhat, he continued, with scathing irony:

"*And now you give this best man of our class the silence, and seek to remove him from the presidency of the class!*"

"It's a shame!" roared another cadet.

There were cheers.

"It is a shame," cried Anstey in a ringing voice. "And now you seek to deepen the shame by further degrading Prescott, who has always been the champion of our class. Mr. President, I move that we lay the motion on the table indefinitely. As soon as that has been done I shall make another motion, that we remove the silence from the grand, good fellow who has had it put upon him."

There were others, however, with nearly Anstey's gift for oratory. One of them now took the floor, pointing out that the class would not have rebuked Prescott for having reported Jordan in the tour of pontoon bridge construction.

"That may have been justified," continued the speaker. "But, afterwards, Mr. Jordan and Mr. Prescott had words. There must have been some bitterness in that. That same night Mr. Jordan was caught and reported by Mr. Prescott, who was not cadet officer of the day, and who therefore must have deliberately shadowed Mr. Jordan in order to catch him."

"Prescott did not shadow Mr. Jordan, or do anything of a sneaky nature," shouted Anstey.

"He refused to explain to our class committee how he happened to be on band at just the time to catch Jordan," shouted Durville.

"Then be assured he had a good military, a good soldierly, a good manly reason for his silence," clamored Anstey.

The meeting was an excited one from all points of view. In the end the best that the staunch friends of Dick could secure was that action on the resignation of the class presidency be deferred until a cooler hour, but that the silence be continued for the present.

And so the meeting broke up. Jordan had been dismayed, fearing that Anstey's impassioned speech might result in putting his enemy back into greater popularity than ever.

But now Jordan was reassured. He was satisfied that things were still moving in his direction, and that Prescott's proud spirit would soon lead him into some action that must make the breach with the class wider than ever.

At noon the next day Prescott returned from the second drill of the forenoon. In his absence a mail orderly had been around. An envelope lay on the table addressed to Dick.

"From Laura," he exclaimed in delight.

"That'll cheer you some," smiled Greg.

"Why it's postmarked from New York," continued Dick swiftly. "Whew! She must be headed this way!"

Hurriedly Prescott tore the envelope open.

"It couldn't have happened at a worse time," he muttered, turning white.

"What?"

"Laura, Mrs. Bentley and Belle Meade are in New York, and will reach here this afternoon. Laura says they have learned that there is a hop on to-night, and they are bringing their prettiest frocks."

"Whew! That is a facer!" breathed Greg in perplexity.

"Of course I can't take Laura to the hop."

"You can, if you have the nerve," insisted Greg.

"And I have the nerve!" retorted Dick defiantly. "But how about Laura? She would discover, within a few minutes, that I am on strained terms with the other fellows. That would do worse than spoil her evening."

"Well," demanded Greg thoughtfully, "why do you need to take her to the hop?"

"Because she says that's what the girls have come for."

"Bother! Do you suppose it's you, or the hop, that Laura comes for?"

But Dick, instead of being cheered by this view, turned very white.

29

"I've got to tell her," he muttered hoarsely, "that I'm in eclipse. That the fellows have voted that I am not a fit associate for gentlemen."

"And I'll tell her a heap more," retorted Cadet Holmes. "Dick, do you think either of the girls would go back on you, just because a lot of raw, half-baked cadets have got you sized up wrong? Is that all the faith you have in your friends? And, especially, such a friend as Laura Bentley? Was that the way she acted when you were under charges of cribbing? You were in disgrace, then, weren't you? Did Laura look at you with anything but sympathy in her eyes?"

"No; heaven bless her!"

"Now, see here, Dick. If the girls are up here this evening, we won't take 'em to the hop. Instead, we'll sit out on the north porch at the hotel, with Mrs. Bentley near by. We'll have such a good old talk with the girls as we never could have at a hop."

"Everything in life would be easy, Greg, if you could explain it away," laughed Dick Prescott, but his tone was bitter.

"Well, as you can't take the girls to the hop, with any regard for their comfort, my plan is best of all, isn't it?"

"I——I suppose so."

"So make the best of it, old ramrod. There's nothing so bad that it couldn't be a lot worse."

There was a long tour of work with the field battery guns that afternoon. For once Prescott found his mind entirely off his work. Nor could he rally his senses to his work. He got a low marking, indeed, in the instructor's record for that afternoon's work.

Then, hot, dusty and tired, this detachment of cadets came in from work.

In the visitors' seats, near headquarters, Dick and Greg espied Mrs. Bentley and the girls. How lovely the two latter looked!

The instant that ranks were broken Laura. and Belle were on their feet, glancing eagerly in the direction of their cadets. Dick and Greg had to go over, doff their campaign hats and shake hands with Mrs. Bentley and the girls.

"We've given you a surprise, this time," laughed Laura. "I hope you're pleased."

"Can you doubt it?" asked Dick so absently, so reluctantly, that Laura Bentley shot a swift, uneasy look at the handsome young cadet captain.

"You don't seem over delighted," broke in Belle Meade. "Gracious! I hope we haven't been indiscreet in coming almost unannounced? See here, you haven't invited any other girls to to-night's hop, have you?"

Both girls, flushed and rather uneasy looking, were now eyeing the two ill-at-ease young first classmen.

"No; we haven't invited anyone else. But there's something to be explained," replied Dick lamely. "Greg, you explain, won't you? And you'll all excuse me, won't you, while I hurry away to tog for dress parade?"

Laura's face was almost as white as Dick's had been at noon, as she gazed after the receding Prescott.

Then Greg, in his bluntest way, tried to put it all straight, and quickly, at that.

"Oh, is that all?" asked Belle with a sniff of contempt. "Why couldn't Dick remain and tell us himself? You cadets are certainly cowards in some things—sometimes!"

But the tears were struggling for a front place in Laura's fine eyes.

"Is this 'silence' going to affect Dick very much in his career in the Army?" she asked with emotion.

"Not if his staunchest friends can prevent it," replied Greg almost fiercely. "And old ramrod has a host of friends in his class, at that."

"It's too bad they're not in the majority, then," murmured Miss Meade.

"They will be, in the end," asserted Greg. "We're working things around to that point. You should have heard the fierce row we put up at the class meeting last night."

When it was too late Greg could have bitten his tongue.

"Class meeting?" asked Laura. "Then has there been further action taken?"

Greg nodded, biting his lips.

"What was last night's meeting held for?" persisted Laura.

"To try to oust Dick from the class presidency," confessed Cadet Holmes.

"Did they do it?" quivered Laura Bentley.

"No!"

"Ah! Then the attempt was defeated. Dick is to retain the presidency of his class?"

"Action was deferred," replied Greg in a low voice.

He wished with all his heart he could get away, for he saw that, no matter how he tried to hedge the facts about, these keen-witted girls realized that Dick Prescott's plight was about as black as it could be for a young man who wanted, with all his soul, to remain in the military service of his country.

CHAPTER VII

JORDAN MEETS DISASTER

Belle, with her combination of impulsive temperament, good judgment and bluntness, came to the temporary rescue.

"Greg is trying to conceal the fact that he'll have a desperate rush to get into his dress uniform in time for parade," Miss Meade interposed. "Anyway, there's far more about this matter than we can understand in a moment. Greg, you and Dick can call on us at the hotel this evening, can't you?"

"We most surely can."

"Then come, as early as you can. We'll eat the earliest dinner we can get there, and be prepared for a long evening. Now, hurry to your tent, for I don't want to see you reported for being late at formation."

Between her visits to West Point, and her trips to Annapolis to see Dave Darrin, as related in the Annapolis Series, Belle had by this time a very considerable knowledge of formations, and of other incidents in the lives of Army and Navy cadets.

"This evening, then," replied Greg, shifting his campaign hat to the other hand and feeling like a man who has secured a reprieve.

"And give my love to Dick," Belle went on hastily, "and tell him that the President of the United States couldn't, if he wanted to, change our opinion of dear old Dick in the least."

"Thank you," bowed Greg, gratitude welling up in his heart.

"And you send him your love, don't you, Laura?" insisted Belle swiftly.

Laura recoiled quickly, flushing violently.

It was all right for Belle Meade to send her "love" to Prescott, for they were old friends, and Belle was known to be Dave Darrin's loyal sweetheart.

With Laura the situation was painfully different. She and Dick had been schoolboy and schoolgirl sweethearts, after a fashion, but Dick had never openly declared his love for her.

Would he misunderstand, and think her unwomanly?

She trembled with the sudden doubt at the thought.

Besides, another, a prosperous young merchant back in Gridley, had been ardent in his attentions to Miss Bentley.

"Of course Laura sends her love," broke in Greg promptly. "Who wouldn't, when the dear old fellow is in such a scrape? And I'll deliver the message of love from you both—-and from Mrs. Bentley, too?"

Greg looked inquiringly, but expectantly at Laura's mother, who nodded and smiled in ready sympathy.

Then Greg made his best soldier's bow and hastened off to his chum, whose heart he succeeded in gladdening somewhat while the two made all haste to get ready for parade call.

When the corps marched on to the field that afternoon, Mrs. Bentley and the girls were there among the eager spectators. Dick saw them almost instantly, and his heart bounded within him. It was Laura's mute message of sympathy and hope to him! He held up his head higher, if that were possible, and went through every movement with even more than his usual precision.

As the corps was marching off the field again, however, Dick's heart sank rapidly within him.

"If I have to leave the Army, I can never ask Laura for her love," he groaned wretchedly. "If I go from West Point as anything but a graduate and an officer, I shall have to start life all over again. It will take me years to find my place and get solidly on my feet I could never ask a girl to wait as long as that!"

In the early evening Laura, Belle and Mrs. Bentley were on the veranda near the hotel entrance. Cadets Jordan and Douglass made their appearance. Jordan had obtained official permission to present Douglass to his sister, who was to go to the hop that evening.

"By Jove, there's a spoony femme (pretty girl) over there," breathed Jordan in Douglass' ear. "You don't happen to know her, do you?"

"Why, yes, that's Miss Bentley, and the other is Miss Meade. The chaperon is Miss Bentley's mother," replied Cadet Douglass.

"You know them?" throbbed Jordan, his eyes resting eagerly on Laura's face. "What luck! Present me, old chap!"

So Douglass, who, in some respects, had a bad memory, piloted his classmate over to the ladies and halted.

"Good evening, ladies," greeted Douglass, raising his uniform cap in his most polished manner. "Mrs. Bentley, Miss Bentley, Miss Meade, will you permit me to present my friend and classmate Mr. Jordan?"

Belle, who was nearest, bowed and held out her hand.

But Laura drew herself up haughtily. "Mr. Douglass," she answered coldly, "my apologies to you, but I don't wish to know——Mr. Jordan!"

Belle caught the name again, and remembered.

"Oh!" she cried, snatching her hand away ere Jordan could touch it.

"I'm sorry, ladies," stammered Douglass. But they found themselves confronted by rear views of two shapely pairs of young shoulders, while Mrs. Bentley had the air of looking through the young men without being able to see either.

Two very much disconcerted cadets, and very red in the face, stiffly resumed their caps and marched away.

"Great Scott, what did that mean?" gasped Jordan, struck all in a heap by his strange reception.

Cadet Douglass gasped.

"Jordan," he exclaimed contritely, "I'm the greatest ass in the corps!"

"You must be!" exploded Dick's enemy. "But what was the cause of it all?"

"Why, Jordan, you——-you see——-"

"Who is Miss Bentley?"

"Jordan, she's Prescott's girl!"

"What?" gasped the other cadet, staring at his classmate.

"Fact!"

"Prescott's——-girl?"

"Yes."

"Jove, a puppy like Prescott has no business with a superb girl like that."

"All the same, Jordan, the fact will prevent you from knowing her."

"Now, I'm not so sure of that!" cried Jordan suddenly, with strange fire in his eyes.

"What do you mean?"

"Oh, nothing," mumbled Jordan, suddenly recovering himself.

Then, under his breath, he chuckled gleefully:

"Miss Bentley is just struck on the uniform, of course. A girl like that couldn't care for a misfit like Prescott. Well, he won't be in the uniform much longer. I won't lose sight of Miss Bentley. I'll find her again when Prescott is out of the uniform for good!"

Now, aloud, he asked:

"Doug, do you happen to remember Miss Bentley's first name?"

"Larry," answered Cadet Douglass absently.

"Stop that!" cried Jordan almost fiercely.

"Oh, a thousand pardons, Jordan. I'm so rattled I don't know what I'm doing or saying. The girl's first name is Laura. Peach, isn't she?"

"Laura! That's a sweet name," murmured Jordan to himself. His mind was now running riot, not only with plans to drive Dick Prescott out of the Army, but also to win the heart of Laura Bentley.

"Hold on, Jord," begged Douglass, halting and leaning against a post in the veranda structure. "Don't take me to your sister just yet. Let me get my breath, my nerves, my wits back again."

"Take an hour," advised Jordan laconically. "You need it. Didn't you know Miss Bentley was Prescott's girl?"

"Yes; but it had slipped my memory. It's mighty hard, when you come to think of it, to remember the girls of so many hundreds of fellows," explained Cadet Douglass plaintively.

Ten minutes later Dick and Greg appeared, greeting the ladies. Mrs. Bentley assented to their going around to the north side of the porch, whence they could look up the river to the lights of Newburgh.

"We very nearly had an adventure, Dick," laughed Belle.

"Yes?"

"We very nearly shook hands with Mr. Jordan. It was Laura's quick cry that saved me, just in the nick of time, from touching hands with the fellow."

Miss Meade then related their experience, and the discomfiture of Cadets Douglass and Jordan.

"That's just about like Doug," observed Greg Holmes. "I'll bet he never thought until Laura called off the signal for the kick."

"What's that?" demanded Miss Bentley.

"Pardon me," apologized Greg. "I think in football terms altogether too often. But I'm glad Jordan saw the goal and then lost it."

"I think Dick wants to tell us something about the fellow Jordan, and some of the other cadets," Belle hinted.

Between them the chums told the story of how the "silence" had come to be imposed. Prescott did not, however, tell his feminine visitors how he had happened to catch Jordan outside the guard line.

"How did that happen?" asked Laura innocently.

"Now, I'd tell you before I would any one else on earth," protested Dick with warmth, "but I haven't told Greg or anyone else. I had good military reasons, not personal ones."

"Oh!" replied Laura. And, not understanding, she felt more than a little hurt by Dick's failure to answer frankly.

Both girls, however, talked very comfortingly, and Mrs. Bentley very sensibly aided their efforts. All three tried to make it quite plain to Dick Prescott that no amount, or consequence, of lack of understanding by his classmates could make any difference with his standing in their eyes.

Presently Mrs. Bentley consented to the girls strolling down the road between the hotel and cadet barracks. Dick, of course, walked with Laura, while Greg and Belle remained at a discreet, out-of-earshot distance.

At last they stood again by the gateway through the shrubbery at the edge of the hotel grounds.

"Dick———" began Laura hesitatingly.

"Yes?" asked the young cadet captain.

"Dick, no matter how far your classmates push this matter," begged Laura, her eyes big and earnest, "don't let their acts force you out of the Army. No matter what happens——stick!"

Cadet Prescott shook his head wearily. "I can't stick," he replied firmly, "if I am shown that my presence in the Army is not going to be for the good and the harmony of the service!"

Laura sighed. Another keen pang of disappointment, was hers.

She now believed that her influence over Dick Prescott was not anywhere near as strong as she had hoped it would be.

A very wretched girl rested her head on a pillow that night, and slept but poorly.

In the forenoon, while the corps was absent on an infantry practice march, Laura, her mother and her friend went dejectedly away from West Point.

CHAPTER VIII

FATE SERVES DICK HER MEANEST TRICK

The furloughed second class returned, the encampment ended and the corps marched back into cadet barracks.

The new academic year had begun, with new text-books, new studies, new intellectual torments for the hundreds of ambitious young soldiers at the United States Military Academy.

By this time both Dick and Greg had acquired the habits of study so thoroughly that neither any longer feared for his standing or markings.

To Prescott there was one big comfort about being back in the old, gray cadet barracks.

The silence put upon Dick was not now quite as much in evidence. With long study hours, Prescott had not so much need to meet his classmates.

In the section rooms nothing in the deportment of the other cadets could emphasize the silence.

It was only in the authorized visiting hours that Prescott noted the change keenly.

Of course, according to the traditions of the Military Academy, Anstey and all the other loyal friends who ached to call were barred from so doing.

While taps sounds at ten o'clock, and members of the three lower classes must be in bed, with lights out, at the first sound of taps, first classmen are privileged, whenever they wish, to run a light until eleven at night, provided the extra time be spent in study.

One evening in early September, Dick and Greg were both busy at study table, when Dick chanced to look over some papers connected with his studies. As he did so, he drew out an officially backed sheet, and started.

"Jupiter!" he muttered. "I should have turned this in before supper formation."

"Who gets the report?" asked Greg, looking up.

"It goes to the officer in charge," Dick answered.

"Oh, well, he's up yet. You can slip over to his office with it," replied Greg easily.

"And I'll do it at once. It may mean a demerit or two, for lack of punctuality, but I'm glad it's no worse."

Jumping up and donning his fatigue cap, Prescott thrust the neglected official report into the breast of his uniform blouse, soldier fashion.

Then he walked slowly out, halting just inside the subdivision door.

"I don't mind a few demerits, but I don't like to be accused of unsoldierly neglect," mused the young cadet captain. "Let me see if I can think up a way of presenting my statement so that the O.C. won't scorch me."

As Dick stood there in the gloom, a quick, soft step sounded outside. Then the door was carefully opened, and a young man in citizen's dress entered.

Civilians rarely have a right, to be in cadet barracks at any time of the day. It is wholly out of the question for one to enter barracks after taps.

"What are you doing in here, sir?" Dick questioned sternly, putting out his hand to take the other's arm.

Then the young cadet captain drew back in near-horror.

"Good heavens! Durville?" he gasped.

"Yes. Sh!" whispered the other cadet, slinking back, a frightened look in his eyes.

No cadet, while at West Point, may, without proper permission, appear in any clothing save the uniform of the day or of the tour. No cadet ever attempts to don "cits." unless he is up to some grave mischief, such as leaving the post.

"Don't say a word! Let me reach my room!" whispered Durville hoarsely.

Dick Prescott wished, with all his heart, to be able to comply with the other cadet's frenzied request.

But duty stepped in with loud voice. As a cadet officer, as captain of Durville's company, Prescott had no alternative within the lines of that duty. He must report Cadet Durville.

"Now, don't look at me so strangely," begged Durville. "Let me go by, and tell me you'll keep this quiet. By Jove, Prescott, you know what it means to me if I'm placed on report for——-this!"

"Yes, I know," nodded Dick, dejectedly, and speaking as hoarsely as did the other man. "Oh, Durville, I wish I could do it, but——-"

Dick had to clench his fists and gulp hard. Then the soldier in him triumphed.

"Mr. Durville"——-he spoke in an impassive official tone, now——-"you will accompany me to the office of the officer in charge, and will there make such official explanation as you may choose."

"Prescott, for the love of——-" began the other over again, in trembling desperation.

"About face, Mr. Durville. Forward!"

Now, all the gameness in the other cadet came to the surface. He wheeled about, head up, his clenched fists seeking the seams of his condemning "cit." trousers. Durville marched defiantly out into the quadrangle, across and into the cadet guard house, up the flight of stairs and into the office of the officer in charge.

Lieutenant Denton was again O.C. that night.

Both cadets saluted when they entered after knocking.

36

Lieutenant Denton glanced in sheer dismay at the "cit." clothes worn by Durville.

"Sir," began Dick huskily, "I regret being obliged to report that I just discovered Mr. Durville entering the sub-division in citizen's dress."

"Have you any explanation to offer, Mr. Durville?" asked Lieutenant Denton in his official tone.

"None, sir."

"Very good, Mr. Durville. You will go to your room and remain in close arrest until you receive further official communication in this matter."

"Very good, sir."

Durville spoke in steady, if icy tones, as he saluted and made this response.

"That is all, Mr. Durville."

"Very good, sir."

Like one frozen, the cadet in unfamiliar attire turned and left the office.

"How did you happen to make the discovery, Mr. Prescott?" gasped the O.C.

"I discovered, sir, that I had overlooked this report, which I now turn in, sir," Dick replied rather hoarsely. "It was just as I was about to leave the sub-division that Mr. Durville came in. I had no alternative but to report him, sir."

"You are right, Mr. Prescott. As a cadet officer you had no alternative."

Then, with a memory of his own West Point days, Lieutenant Denton unbent enough to remark feelingly:

"You have unassailable courage, too, Mr. Prescott."

"Thank you, sir."

"Is that all?"

"You have finished your official business?"

"Yes, sir."

"Good night," Mr. Prescott.

"Good night, sir."

Saluting, Dick turned from the office. As he pushed open the door and reentered the subdivision, he beheld Durville, standing there with arms folded.

"Possibly at the risk of being reported for breaking my arrest, Mr. Prescott," began Durville, "I have lingered here to say to you that you have succeeded in wreaking a most complete revenge upon one who led a bit in having the silence conferred upon you."

All Dick's reserve melted for an instant.

"Durville, man——you——don't believe I did this for——for revenge?" Prescott demanded.

Cadet Durville smiled sarcastically.

"I shall undoubtedly be broken for this night's affair, Mr. Prescott, and you and the rest will continue to believe that I was absent merely on some vulgar escapade! I go, now, to my arrest, which is doubtless the last military service I shall be called upon to render. Mr. Prescott, I congratulate you, sir, upon your ability to spy upon other men and to serve your highest ideas of suitable vengeance."

Gloomily Durville turned to his room. Dick almost stumbled to his own quarters.

Greg Holmes's face blanched when he heard the news.

"There'll be fine class ructions by to-morrow!" he told himself with unwonted grimness.

CHAPTER IX

THE CLASS TAKES FINAL ACTION

By the time the corps of cadets was seated at breakfast, in the great mess hall, the following morning, the news began to circulate rapidly.

It was discussed in low tones at every table save that at which the silence against Prescott prevailed.

The silence by this time had ceased to be literal, except so far as it applied to Dick. Other cadets at his table talked among themselves, though never to Prescott. Greg, being Dick's roommate, was the sole cadet exempted from this rule.

But the men at Prescott's table restrained their curiosity until the two battalions had marched back to barracks and had been dismissed.

After the dismissal of the companies Dick and Greg strolled along slowly. Wherever they passed backs were turned to them, though this would not have happened to Holmes had he been alone.

Though the news was discussed, no class action was taken. This must not be done until Durville's fate had overtaken him. Otherwise, the Military Academy authorities might take such action as defiant and visit a more severe penalty upon Cadet Durville.

For five days Durville remained in close arrest. This meant, to the initiated, that the Superintendent had taken up the matter with the War Department at Washington.

On the sixth day Durville was once more sent for by the commandant of cadets. His sentence was handed out to him. On account of an academic reputation of high grade, and a hitherto good-conduct report, Mr. Durville was not dropped from the corps. Had the offender, before leaving West Point in "cits.," gone to the cadet guard house and made any false report concerning his absence, nothing could have saved him from dismissal for making a false official report. All things being taken into consideration, Cadet Durville was "let off" with loss of privileges up to the time of semi-annual examinations, with, in addition, the walking of punishment tours every Saturday afternoon during the same period.

Now the gathering wrath broke loose upon Dick. A class meeting was called, that neither Prescott nor Holmes could attend with propriety.

Durville, as a matter of policy, did not attend, but there were not wanting first classmen who looked upon Durville as a sacrifice, and who were fully capable of presenting his side of the case at the meeting.

Upon Anstey, as on a former occasion, fell the task of making Prescott's side clear.

The class meeting had not been in session many minutes when Dick's accusers had made it rather plain that Mr. Prescott, following his previous course with Jordan, had revenged himself also on Durville, who had taken an active part in securing the imposition of the silence.

Anstey took the floor in a fiery defence. He brought forth the statement that Prescott had not made any attempt to pry into the goings or comings of the unlucky Durville. The Virginian declared that Prescott had happened to be abroad in time to "catch" Mr. Durville, simply because Prescott had started for the office of the officer in charge with an official paper that he had been tardy about turning in.

Though Anstey dwelt upon this side of the case with consummate oratory, the defence was regarded as "too transparent." Anstey's good faith was not questioned, but Prescott's was.

In the turmoil the office of class president was declared vacant. Anstey was nominated for the office just made vacant, but, with cold politeness, he refused what, at any other time, would have been a high honor.

Cadet Douglass was presently elected class president.

Then further action was taken with regard to Cadet Richard Prescott. Without further debate a motion was carried that Prescott be sent to Coventry for good and all.

The class meeting adjourned, and upon Greg Holmes, who was informed by Anstey, fell the task of carrying the decision to Dick.

"I expected it, Holmesy," was Dick's quiet reply.

"Buck up, anyway, old ramrod," begged Greg. "This terrible mess will all be straightened out before graduation."

"Not in time to do me any good," replied Dick gloomily.

"Now what do you mean?"

But Dick closed his jaws firmly.

Greg knew better than to press his questioning further, just then. He contented himself with crossing the room, resting both hands on Dick's shoulders.

"Now, old ramrod, just remember this: Into every life a good deal of trouble comes. It is up to each fellow, in his own case, to show how much of a man he is. The fellow who lies down, or runs away, isn't a man. The fellow who fights his trouble out to a grim finish, is a man every inch of his five or six feet! The class is wild, just now, but on misinformation. Fight it out! Enemies of yours have brought you to this pass. Don't run away! All your friends are with you as much as ever they were."

Dick was a good deal affected.

"Believe me, Greg, whatever I decide on doing won't be in the line of running away. Whatever I decide upon will be what I finally believe to be for the best good of the service."

"Humph!" muttered Greg, looking wonderingly at his chum.

In the closing period of the next forenoon Dick's section did not recite. Greg's did. So Prescott was left alone in the room with his books.

Despite himself, Greg was so worried, during that recitation, that he "fessed cold"——that is, he secured a mark but a very little above zero.

As soon as the returning section was dismissed Cadet Holmes, his heart beating fast, hurried to his room.

There sat Dick, at the study table, as Greg had left him. But Prescott had pushed his textbooks aside. Before him rested only a sheet of paper. With pen in hand Prescott wrote something at the bottom just as Holmes entered the room. Then Dick looked up with a half cheery face.

"I've done it, Greg," he announced simply, in a hard, dry voice.

"Done it?" echoed Cadet Holmes. "What?"

"I have written my resignation as a member of the corps of cadets, United States Military Academy."

"Bosh!" roared Cadet Holmes in a great rage. "The resignation is written, signed, and——it sticks!" returned Dick Prescott with quiet emphasis.

CHAPTER X

LIEUTENANT DENTON'S STRAIGHT TALK

"Let me have that paper!" demanded Greg, darting forward.

There was fire in Cadet Holmes's eyes and purpose in his heart as he reached forward to snatch the sheet from the desk.

Yet Dick Prescott stepped before him, thrusting him quietly aside with a manner that was not to be overridden.

"Don't touch it, Greg!" he ordered in a low voice that was none the less compelling.

"But you shan't send that resignation in!" quivered Greg.

"My dear boy, you know very well that I shall!"

"Have you no thought for me?" Cadet Holmes demanded.

"My going may put you in a blue streak for a week, old fellow, but it will put me in a blue streak for a lifetime. Yet there's no other way for me. What's the use of being an ostracized officer in the service? With you, Greg, old chum, it is different. You will, after a little, be very happy in the Army."

"Happy in the——nothing!" exploded Greg. "I told you, weeks ago, that if you quit the service, I would do the same thing."

"But you won't," urged Dick. "In these weeks you have had time to reflect and turn sensible."

"Do you suppose I care to go on, old chum, if you don't?"

"Yes," answered Dick quietly. "And if the case were reversed, and you were resigning, I should go on just the same and stick in the service. Why, Greg, if we both went on into the Army, and under the happiest conditions, we wouldn't be together, anyway. You might be in one regiment, down in Florida, and I in another out in the Philippines. When I was serving in Cuba, you'd be in Alaska. Don't be foolish, Greg. I've got to leave, but there's no earthly reason why you should. Your resigning would be mistaken loyalty to me, and would cast no rebuke or regret over the cadet corps or the Army. The fellows who are going to stick would simply feel that one weak-kneed chap had dropped by the wayside. They'd merely march on and forget you."

"There goes the first call for dinner formation," cried Holmes, wheeling and beginning his hasty preparations.

"That's better," laughed Dick, as he shoved his resignation into the drawer of the table.

Then Dick, too, made his hurried preparations. Second call found them ready to watch the forming of A company. At the command Dick gave his own company order:

"Fours right! Forward——march!"

Away went A company, at the head of the corps, the whole long line giving forth the rhythmic sound of marching feet.

No outsider could have guessed that the young senior cadet captain was utterly discredited by the majority of his class, and that he was about to drop hopelessly out of this stirring life.

On the return from dinner Dick went at once to his room.

"What are you going to do?" demanded Greg impatiently, as Prescott seated himself at the study table.

"I am going to address an envelope to hold the sheet of paper of which you so much disapprove."

Greg knew it was useless to expostulate. Instead, he hurried out, found Anstey, and called the Virginian so that both could stand in the place where they would be sure to see Prescott if he attempted to come out.

Feverishly, in undertones, Greg confided the news to Anstey.

"I don't just see what we can do, suh," answered the southerner with a puzzled look.

"Prescott is doing, suh, just what I reckon I'd do myself, suh, if I were in his place."

"But we can't lose him," urged Greg.

"I know we'll hate like thunder to, suh. But what can we do? Can we beg Prescott to stay, and face the cold shoulder, suh, all the time he is here, and in the Army afterwards?"

"I'm not getting much comfort out of you, Anstey," muttered Greg grimly.

"And that, suh, is because I don't see where the comfort comes in. Holmesy, don't think I'm not suffering, suh. It'll break my heart to see old ramrod drop out of the corps."

"Then you don't think we can stop Prescott?"

"I reckon I don't Holmesy. This is the kind of matter, suh, that every man must settle for himself. If I were a much older man, Holmesy, with much more experience in the Army, I reckon I might be able to give him some very sound advice. But as it is, suh, I know I can't."

When Greg returned to the room he found Dick preparing books and papers to march to the next section recitation.

"What have you done with that resignation of yours?" growled Greg.

"It's in that drawer," replied Dick, with a weary smile, "and I rely on you, old fellow, not to do anything to it. It would only give me all the pain over again if I had to rewrite it."

"Dick, can nothing change your mind?"

"I have thought it all over, old friend."

The call for section formation sounded, and both hurried away.

Later, Dick's section returned a full minute and a half ahead of the one to which Holmes belonged.

"Now's the time!" muttered Dick, opening the drawer and slipping the envelope into the breast of his blouse.

41

Then he hurried out, crossing the quadrangle to the cadet guard house. Cadet Holmes, in section ranks, marched into the quadrangle in time just to catch a glimpse of Prescott's disappearing back.

Going up the stairs, Dick knocked on the door of the office of the O.C.

"Come in!" called the officer in charge, who proved to be none other than Lieutenant Denton again.

"What is it, Mr. Prescott?" inquired the Army officer, as Prescott, saluting, advanced to the officer's desk, then halted, standing at attention.

"Sir, I have come to ask for some information."

"What is it, Mr. Prescott?"

"Sir, I have a paper, addressed to the superintendent. I do not know whether I should take it to the adjutant's office, or whether I should forward it through this office."

"I thought you understood your company paper work, Mr. Prescott," smiled Lieutenant Denton.

"I think I do, sir; but this kind of paper I have never had to put in before."

"What kind of paper is it?"

"My resignation, sir," replied Dick quietly. Lieutenant Denton looked almost as much astonished as he felt.

"What?" he choked. Then a slight smile came into his face.

"Oh, I think I begin to understand, Mr. Prescott. You wish more time for your studies, and so you are resigning your post as captain of A company."

"This is my resignation, sir, from the corps of cadets."

Lieutenant Denton looked utterly nonplussed.

"Oh, very good, Mr. Prescott. If you are bent on leaving the Military Academy, I presume I have no right to demand your reasons. But——won't you sit down?"

The lieutenant pointed to a chair near his own.

"Thank you, sir," nodded Prescott. Taking off his fatigue cap, he dropped into the chair, though he sat very erect.

"Now," smiled Mr. Denton, "perhaps we can drop, briefly, some of the relation between officer and cadet. We may be able to talk as friends——real friends. I trust so. May I feel at liberty to ask you, Mr. Prescott, whether there are any urgent family reasons behind this sudden move of yours?"

"None, sir."

"Then is it——but I don't wish to be intrusive."

"I certainly don't consider you intrusive, Mr. Denton, and I appreciate your sympathy and friendship. But I am resigning from the corps for the best of good reasons."

"May I question you, Mr. Prescott?"

"If you care to, sir."

"I do wish it, very much," rejoined Lieutenant Denton, "though I have asked your consent because, in what I am now seeking to do, I am going rather beyond my place as a tactical officer of the Military Academy. If you are sure, however, that you do not find me intrusive, and if you would like to talk this matter over—not as officer and cadet, but as between a young man and a somewhat older one, and as friends above all, then I am going to ask you a few questions."

"Although I am certain that you cannot help me, Mr. Denton, I am very grateful for every sign of interest that you may show in me. It is something of balm to me to feel that I shall leave behind some who will regret my going."

"Prescott," asked the officer abruptly, "you have been sent to Coventry, haven't you? You needn't answer unless you wish."

"I have, sir," Dick assented.

"Twice it has happened, when I have been on duty, that you have had to report classmates to me. Now, I'm not going to step over the line by asking you whether those reports were the basis of your being sent to Coventry. But, to please myself, I'm going to assume that such is the case."

To this Dick made no reply. It was an instance in which a cadet could not, with propriety, discuss class action with an officer on duty at the Military Academy.

"Now, Prescott, I'm not going to ask you whether my surmise is a correct one, but I'm going to ask you another question, as a friend only, and in no official way. Of course, in a friendly matter you may suit yourself about answering it. Have you done anything else that could excuse the class in punishing you?"

"Nothing whatever, sir."

"Mr. Prescott, aren't you wholly satisfied with your conduct?"

"I don't quite know how to answer that, Mr. Denton,"

"Have you done anything that you wouldn't repeat if the need arose?"

"I have not, sir," replied Dick with great earnestness.

"Do you feel, in your own soul, that you have done anything to discredit the splendid old gray uniform that you wear?"

"I do not, sir."

"Answer this, or not, as you please. Don't you feel wholly convinced that your class has done you an injustice which it would reverse instantly if it knew all the circumstances?"

"I feel certain that my classmates would restore me at once to their favor, if they knew the full circumstances."

"Have you felt obliged to refuse them any information for which a class committee had asked, Prescott?"

"Yes, sir."

"Let me do some hard thinking, my lad. Ah, now, as I look back to the night when you were obliged to report Mr. Jordan for being outside the guard lines, I had myself that night assigned you to official duty near the guard lines. You were to intercept plebes who might try to run the guard, and to send them back to their tents."

"Yes, sir."

"That was special duty," resumed Lieutenant Denton. "Now, if you had been asked, by a class committee, to explain how you happened to be out there at the right time to catch Mr. Jordan, you would have felt bound to refuse to reveal your orders from me?"

"I certainly would have felt so bound, Mr. Denton."

43

"Ah! Now I think I understand a good deal, Prescott. Then, at another time, very recently, you forgot, until late, to turn in an official report to me. You started to hurry over here, and, in so doing, you must have accidentally encountered a certain cadet returning in "cit." clothes. As his company commander, you surely felt bound to report him for so flagrant a breach of discipline. Yet, if your class did not fully understand or credit the fact that only an oversight of yours had thrown you in that cadet's way, it would make the class feel that you had deliberately trapped the man, after having spied on his actions earlier in the evening."

Dick remained silent, but Lieutenant Denton was a clear headed and logical guesser.

"In my cadet days," smiled the lieutenant, "such a suspicion against a cadet officer would certainly have resulted in ostracism for him."

"Now, Prescott," asked the officer in charge, leaning over and resting a friendly hand on the cadet's arm, "you feel that you have been, throughout, a gentleman and a good soldier, and that you have not done anything sneaky?"

"That is my opinion of myself, Mr. Denton."

"And yet, feeling that your course has been wholly honorable, you are going to throw up your career in the Army, and waste some twenty thousand dollars of the nation's money that has been expended in giving you your training here?"

"It sounds like a fearful thing to do, Mr. Denton, but I can see no way out of it, sir. If I am to go on into the Army, and be an ostracized officer, I should be of no value to myself or to the service. Wherever I should go, my usefulness would be gone and my presence demoralizing."

"Now, if that ostracism continued, your usefulness would be gone, Prescott, beyond a doubt, and the Army would be better off without you. But if justice should triumph, later, you would be restored to your full usefulness, and to the full enjoyment of your career. Now, Prescott, my boy"—-here the officer's voice became tender, friendly, earnest—-"you have been attending chapel every Sunday?"

"Yes, sir."

"You have listened to the chaplain's discourses, and I take it that you have had earlier religious instruction, also. Prescott, do you or do you not believe that there is a God above who sees all, loves all and rights all injustice in His own good time?"

"Assuredly I believe it, sir."

"And yet, in your own case, you have so little faith in that justice that, though you feel your course has been honorable, you cannot wait for justice to be done. Prescott, isn't that kind of faith almost blasphemy?"

Dick felt staggered. Although his lot had been cast with Army officers for more than three years, he had never heard any of them, save the chaplain, discuss matters of Christian faith. Yet he knew that Denton, who sat beside him, smiling with friendly eyes, was talking from full conviction.

"You've made me see my present predicament in a somewhat different light, sir," Dick stammered.

"Prescott, I have knocked about in a good deal of rough life since I was graduated from here, but I have full faith that every upright and honorable man is ultimately safe under Heaven's justice. So have you, or I am mistaken in you. Why not buck up, and make up your mind to go through your hard rub here firm in the conviction that this is only a passing cloud that is certain to be dispelled? Why not stick, like a man of faith and honor? Now, as officer in charge, I will inform you that you should take a letter of resignation to the adjutant's office, and hand it to that officer in person."

As your friend, I suggest that you give me your letter, with your permission to destroy it."

"Here is the letter, Mr. Denton."

"Thank you, my boy. You may see what I do with it."

Rising, Lieutenant Denton crossed to an open fire that was burning low. He laid the envelope across the embers.

Prescott, too, rose, feeling that the interview was at an end.

"Just a moment more of friendly conversation, Prescott," continued the lieutenant, coming forward and taking the cadet's hand. "I want you to remember that you are not to write or send in any other letter of resignation until you have first talked it over with me. And I want you to remember that a soldier should be a man of faith as well as of honor. Further, Prescott, you may feel yourself wholly at liberty to explain, at any time, what your orders from me were that led to your catching and reporting Mr. Jordan."

"Thank you, sir; but I'm afraid I shan't be asked for any further explanations."

"Seek me, at any time, if there is anything you wish to ask me, or anything that puzzles you."

"Yes, sir; thank you."

Dick had again placed his fatigue cap on his head, and was standing rigidly at attention. They were once more tactical officer and cadet.

"That is all, Mr. Prescott, and I am very glad that you came to see me," continued the officer in charge.

Prescott saluted, received the officer's acknowledging salute, turned and left the office.

A minute later he was allowing good old Greg to pump the details of that interview out of him.

"Say," muttered Cadet Holmes, staring soberly at his chum, "an officer like Lieutenant Denton can put a different look on things, can't be?"

"He certainly can, Greg."

"I'm not going to be fresh, while I'm a cadet," continued Holmes. "But when I'm an officer I'm going to seek Mr. Denton and ask him to be my friend, too!"

CHAPTER XI

THE NEWS FROM FRANKLIN FIELD

Though Dick was firmly resolved on his new course, life none the less was bitter for him.

The Army football team was now being organized and drilled in earnest. Douglass captained it this year, and was doing excellent work, though his material was not as good as he could have wished.

45

Anstey was developing speed and strategy in the position of quarterback, and, in football matters, was a close confidant of Douglass.

"This Prescott muss has given us a bad setback this year," growled Douglass.

"It certainly has, suh," agreed the Virginian. "We're certainly going to feel the loss of Prescott and Holmes when we come to face the Navy eleven with such men as Darrin and Dalzell."

"Hang it, yes. I'm shivering already," growled Douglass. "Now, of course, we can't ask Prescott to join."

"And he wouldn't come in, suh, while in Coventry, if we asked him."

"But Holmes, who is almost as good a man, ought not to hold back where the Army's credit and honor are at stake. Holmes ought to stand for the Army, asleep or awake!"

"If I were in Holmesy's place, I wouldn't come in," rejoined the Virginian. "I'd stay out, just as Holmesy is doing."

"But you were one of Prescott's thick friends, too."

"I'm not his roommate, or his schoolboy chum, suh. Holmesy is.

"It's hard to lose either of them," sighed Douglass, "and fierce to lose both of them. We've worked like real heroes, but I can't see any such team coming on as the Army had last year. And the Navy eleven will undoubtedly be better this year than it was last."

"The Army must stand to lose by the action of the first class," insisted Anstey doggedly.

Though every man in the corps would have thrown up his cap at the announcement that Prescott and Holmes were to play again this year, the leaders of first-class opinion could see no reason to alter their judgment of Dick. So he continued in Coventry.

The football season came on with a rush at last. The Army won some of its games, from minor teams, but none from the bigger college elevens.

Then came the fateful Saturday when the corps went over to Philadelphia. Dick and Greg were the only two members of the corps, not under severe discipline, who remained behind at the Military Academy.

Late that afternoon Greg, with a long face, brought in the football news from Franklin Field.

"The Navy has wiped us up, ten to two," grumbled Holmes.

"I'm heartily sorry," cried Dick, and he spoke the truth.

"Well, it's our class's fault," growled Greg. "The Army can thank our class."

"We might not have been able to save the game," argued Prescott.

"We could have rattled Dave and Dan a lot," retorted Greg. "My own belief is we could have saved the day."

"You might have played, Greg. I wouldn't have resented it."

"No; but I'd have felt a fine contempt for myself," retorted Cadet Holmes scornfully. "Besides, Dick, though I have done some fairly good things in football, I don't believe I'd be worth a kick without you. It was playing with you that made me shine, always."

46

Late that evening the cadet corps returned, in the gloomiest frame of mind.

"I can just see the blaze of bonfires at Annapolis," groaned Douglass. "Say, the middies just fairly tore our scalps off. I always had an ambition to captain the Army eleven, but I never thought I'd be dragged down so deep under the mire!"

The details of that sad game for the Army need not be gone into here. All the particulars of that spiritedly fought disaster will be found in the fourth volume of the Annapolis Series, entitled *"Dave Darrin's Fourth Year At Annapolis."*

A lot of the cadets who felt sorry for "Doug" came to his room.

"I haven't altogether gotten it through my weak mind yet," confessed the disheartened Army football captain. "I can't understand how those little middies managed to treat us quite so badly."

"I can tell you," retorted Anstey.

"Then I wish you would," begged "Doug."

"Go ahead!" clamored a dozen others.

"I don't know whether you fellows believe in hoodoos?" asked Anstey.

"Hoodoos?"

"Yes; the Army is under one now."

"Pshaw, Anstey!"

"Explain yourself, Anstey!"

"There is a man in this class," replied the Virginian solemnly, "who has been treated unjustly by the others. Lots of you won't see it, and can't be made to reason. But that injustice has put the hoodoo on the Army's athletics, and the hoodoo will strut along beside the present first class all the way through this year. You'll find it out more and more as time goes on. Just wait until next spring, and see the Navy walk away with the baseball game, too."

"Stop that, Anstey!"

"Put him out!"

"Give him soothing syrup."

"Wait until June, gentlemen," retorted the Virginian calmly.

"Then you'll see."

"What rot!" sneered Jordan bitterly.

"Well, of course," admitted others in undertones, "we lost through not having Prescott and Holmes on the eleven. But we'd better lose, even, than win through men not fit to associate with."

"Prescott must be chuckling," jeered Durville.

"He's doing nothing of the sort, suh!" flared Anstey. "And I'm prepared to maintain my position."

CHAPTER XII

READY TO BREAK THE CAMEL'S BACK

From Thanksgiving to Christmas the time seemed to fly all too fast for most of the young men of the corps of cadets.

Dick Prescott, however, had never known time to drag so fearfully. Cut off from association with any but Greg, Dick had much, very much time on his hands.

Full of a dogged purpose to stick to his word given to Lieutenant Denton, Prescott used nearly all of his waking time in study when he was not at recitation. In his classes he soared. In engineering and law, the studies of this term which called for the most exacting thought, Prescott showed unusual signs of "maxing," or getting among the highest marks. Yet, after all this was done, so much leisure did the lonely Dick have that he found time to coach Greg and pull him along over the hard parts.

"Look at that fellow recite! Look where he stands in the sections!" growled Durville in bewilderment to Jordan.

"It looks as if the sneak meant to stick," uttered Jordan incredulously.

"Yet of course he knows he can't. If it were only for West Point he might stick, but the Army, through his lifetime, would be just as bad for him."

It had been a general notion that Prescott, either too proud or too stubborn to allow himself to be forced out, would wait and "fess out cold" at the January semi-annuals. Thus he would be dropped for deficiency, and would not have to admit to anyone that he had allowed himself to be driven from the Military Academy by the "silence" that had been extended to him.

Jordan knew better than to go near the fiery young Anstey, so he managed to induce Durville to speak to the Virginian as to Prescott's plans.

"I don't know Mr. Prescott's intentions, suh," replied Anstey with perfect truth and a good deal of dignity. "I am bound, suh, to follow the class's action, suh, much as I disapprove of it. So I have had no word with Mr. Prescott later than you have."

"But you know the fellow's roommate, Mr. Holmes," suggested Durville.

"I am under the impression that you do, too, suh," replied Anstey significantly, yet without infusing offence into his even tones.

It was no use. The first class could only guess. No cadet knew, unless it were Holmes, what Prescott's intentions were about quitting the corps in the near future. And Greg, usually both chatty and impulsive, could be as cold and silent as a sphinx where his chum's secrets or interests were concerned.

Had he wished, he might have gone home at Christmas, for a day or two, for he was on the good-conduct roll; but Dick felt that Christmas at home would be a heart break just now. As he did not go, Greg did not go either.

The reader may be sure that Dave Darrin and Dan Dalzell, at Annapolis, knew the state of affairs with their old-time friend and leader. Greg had sent word of what was happening with Dick.

"Buck up——that's all, old chap," Dave wrote from the Naval Academy. "You never did a mean thing, and you never will. Even your class will learn that before very long. So buck up! Hit the center of the line and charge through! Don't think Dan and I are not sorry for you, but we're even more interested in seeing you charge right through all disaster in a way that fits the pride, courage and honor that we know you to possess. I asked Dan if he had any message to send you. Old Dan's reply was: 'Dick doesn't need any message. If there's any fellow on earth who can jump in and scalp Fate, it's our old Dick.' There you are, Army chum! We're merely waiting for word that you've won out, for you're bound to."

January came, and with it the semi-annual examinations. So high was Dick's class standing that he had to go up for but one "writ." That was Spanish.

"I reckon Spanish is where he falls," chuckled Durville, when Jordan spoke to him about it. "It's easy to make mistakes enough on Spanish verbs and declensions to throw a fellow down and out. That'll be Prescott's line."

"Of course," nodded Jordan. Yet Dick's enemy was very far from feeling hopeful that such would be the case.

"I never imagined the fellow could stick as long as he has," Jordan told himself disconsolately.

One night Anstey, just before the semi-ans., took a chance. Usually the Virginian was careful in matters of discipline. But now he invited a dozen members of his class to his room to discuss an "important matter."

"Going?" asked Durville of Jordan.

"I'm not invited, Durry," replied the other.

"I am, and I'm going."

"But you don't know the subject of the meeting?"

"No; that's what puzzles me," admitted Durville. "I'm wondering if it has anything to do with choosing the class ring, or selecting our uniforms for after graduation."

"You simpleton!" cried Jordan in disgust. "You don't see far, do you? Can't you guess what the meeting is to discuss?"

"I'm blessed if I can."

"Anstey, outside of Holmes, has been the most constant friend of Prescott. Now, Prescott has his chance of passing, if the class 'silence' on him can be lifted. Anstey is going to sound class opinion. If the 'silence' can't be lifted, then Prescott is going to 'fess' down and out, and we shall see the last of him."

"Poor old fellow!" muttered Durville. "Say, do you know, I'm growing almost sorry for the poor beggar and his long, bitter dose."

"After what he did to you?" demanded Jordan with instant scorn. "Durville, I thought you a man of spirit."

"May a man of spirit forgive his enemy, especially when he sometimes doubts whether the other fellow really is an enemy?" demanded Durville.

"Oh, he may, I suppose," replied Jordan, his lip curling. "On the whole, however, I am a good deal surprised at seeing you accept the loss of all your liberties and privileges so easily as you are doing."

Naturally, the effect of Jordan's words was to kill a good deal of Durville's fleeting sympathy, for the latter had suffered a good deal from the restraint of his liberties, following the escapade for which Dick had reported him.

The meeting in Anstey's room resulted in the secret gathering of a dozen men. Eight of these were friends of Dick, who would still like to see the class action reversed or ended. But Anstey had been clever enough also to invite four men who were numbered among Prescott's adversaries. One of these was Douglass, the cadet who had been elected to succeed Dick as class president.

"Now, gentlemen," began Anstey, in his soft voice of ordinary conversation, "I don't believe we have any need of a presiding officer in this little meeting. With your permission, I will state why I have asked you to come here.

"For months, now, we have had a member of this class in Coventry. Barely more than a majority believed in that Coventry, but once action had been taken by the class, the disapproving minority stood loyally by class action. I have been among those of the minority to abide by majority action, and I can assure you that I have suffered very nearly as much as has Mr. Prescott, whose case I am now discussing.

"The majority has had its way for months. Is it not now time, if the class will not grant full justice, at least to grant something to the wishes of the minority?"

"What do you mean?" asked one of Dick's opponents. "Mr. Prescott will let himself be found deficient in at least one study, won't he, and thus take his unpopular presence away from the Military Academy?"

"I cannot answer that," admitted Anstey slowly. "Doubtless many of you will be surprised when I tell you that I have had no word in the matter from Mr. Prescott. I have not even mentioned the subject to his roommate, Mr. Holmes."

"Then whom do you represent?" demanded the other cadet.

"Myself and other believers in Mr. Prescott," replied Anstey simply. "The very least we ask is that you stop punishing so many of us through Mr. Prescott. Gentlemen, do you not feel that any man who commands as many friends in his class as does Mr. Prescott must be a man above the petty meannesses of which he was accused, and for which he was sent to Coventry?"

"I've been one of the sufferers through Mr. Prescott," commented Durville grimly. "As for me, I'll admit that I'd be glad to see the 'silence' lifted. I feel that Mr. Prescott has been punished enough, and that, if we now lift the 'silence,' he would be more careful after this. I think he has been chastened enough. If I could find any reason whatever for refusing to vote for the end of the Coventry, it would come from the question as to whether any one class has the right to upset the traditions and establish a new precedent for such cases."

"There is the most of the case in a nutshell I am afraid," declared Cadet Douglass. "In our interior corps discipline we not only work from tradition, but we strengthen or weaken it for the classes that are to follow us. Have we any right to weaken a tradition that is as old as the Military Academy itself?"

These simple remarks, made with an absence of bitter feeling, swung the tide against Dick. The meeting in Anstey's room lasted for more than an hour. When the meeting broke up Anstey and some of his advisers felt convinced that to call a class meeting would be merely to bring about a vote that Prescott was to be kept in Coventry for all time to come.

Anstey told Greg the result of the meeting, but Holmes did not tell his chum.

"It's all settled as it ought to be," declared Cadet Jordan.

"You mean——" asked Durville.

"Why, either Prescott will have to be 'found' in his exams., or else he'll be bound to resign as soon as he has proved that his departure from West Point was not due to poor scholarship. Which ever way he prefers to do it, the fellow will have to get out of the corps within the next few days!"

"Yes; I suppose so," almost sighed Durville.

"Why, hang you, Durry, you talk like a man whose good opinion can be won by a kicking."

"Do you" asked Durville, with a warning flash in his eyes.

"Oh, don't take me too seriously," protested Jordan. "But I cannot help marveling at your near liking for the man who landed you in such a scrape."

"I don't enjoy hitting a man who is down; that is all," returned Durville. "I've seen Mr. Prescott down for so many weeks and months that I'd like to see how he looks when he's a man instead of an under dog."

"Well, I'm glad to say the class is plainly not of your way of thinking," growled Jordan. "The class is for maintaining higher ideals of the honor of military service and true comradeship. So it's only a matter of what date the fellow selects for leaving here."

And truly that was the view that seemed to be pressing more and more tightly upon Dick Prescott. The pressure was becoming more than he could bear. He had followed Lieutenant Denton's advice, and had put up a good and a brave fight. But to be "the only dog in a cage of lions" is a fearful ordeal for the bravest—-especially when the door is open.

Greg never seemed to notice the sighs that occasionally escaped Dick Prescott's lips. Holmes no longer tried to cheer his friend by open speech or advice. Yet not a thing that Dick did escaped the covert watchfulness of his roommate.

The semi-ans. over, and the results posted on the bulletin board in the Academic Building, it was discovered that Cadet Richard Prescott now stood number twenty-four in his class—-a rank never heretofore won by him.

Cadet Jordan was so furious that his face was ghastly white when he made the discovery.

"Will nothing ever drive that living disgrace Prescott out of the corps?" Jordan asked three or four of the men. "Why, the fellow is defying class authority! He's making fools of us all. He bluntly asks us what we think we can do about it!"

"We'll have to show Prescott, then," grimly replied one of the cadets with whom Jordan talked.

"But how?" demanded Cadet Jordan craftily. "Is there any possible way of making as thickheaded or stubborn a fellow as Prescott realize that he simply can't go on with us? That we won't have him with us?"

"Oh, I think there's a way," smiled the other cadet.

"Then I wonder why some one doesn't find it?" demanded Jordan wrathfully.

"We shall, I think."

Greg scented new mischief in the air, yet he was hardly the one to do the scouting.

Anstey, however, could look about for the news, and he could properly discuss it with Cadet Holmes.

With the beginning of the last half of the year the members of the first class found themselves sufficiently busy with their studies. Dick's affair was allowed to slumber for a few days.

Even Cadet Jordan, whose sole purpose now in life was to "work" Prescott out of the corps, was clever enough to assent to letting the matter rest for a few days.

After another fortnight, however, the first class, in its moments of leisure, especially in the brief rests right after meals, again began to throb over what was considered the brazen and open defiance of Dick Prescott in persisting in remaining a cadet at the Military Academy.

So many members of the class, however, insisted on going slowly and with great deliberation that the Jordan faction did not make the mistake of rushing matters. At any rate, Prescott was in Coventry, and there he would stay.

Thus February came on and passed slowly. To all outward appearances Prescott was as selfpossessed and contented as ever he had been while at the Military Academy.

Now, Army baseball was the topic. The nine and other members of the baseball squad were practising in earnest. Durville had been chosen to captain the nine.

Though there was some mighty good material in the nine, neither the coaches nor Durville were wholly satisfied.

"Holmesy," broached Durville plaintively one day, "you play a grand game of football."

"Thank you," replied Greg, with a pretense of mock modesty; "I know it."

"And you must play a great game of ball, too."

"I did once—-pardon these blushes. Dick Prescott was my old trainer in baseball."

"Oh, bother Prescott! We can't have him."

"I don't play well without him," remarked Greg blandly.

"Come over to practice this afternoon, won't you?"

"Yes; but I don't believe I'll try for the nine."

"Come over and let us see your style, any way."

Greg turned up late that afternoon for practice. What he showed the captain and coaches had them fairly "rattled" with desire to slip Greg into the nine.

"I'm much obliged to you all," Greg insisted gently, "but I told you I wasn't going to try for the nine. I never played a game without Prescott, and I know I'd be a hoodoo if I did."

Though a great lot of pressure was brought to bear upon him, Holmes still held out. It was his privilege to refuse to play, if he so chose. Above all, the coaches, who were Army officers, could not urge him.

"That man Holmes is just the fellow we need to round out the team," complained one of the players to Durville.

"Yes," sighed the captain of the Army nine; "and Holmesy tells me that he's a tyro to Mr. Prescott."

"Then Mr. Prescott must be a wonder on the diamond," grunted the other cadet.

"I hear that he is," assented Durville. "By the way, you remember Darrin and Dalzell, who helped the Navy team to wipe the field up with us last year?"

"I reckon I do."

"Well, it seems that Prescott, Holmes, Darrin and Dalzell were all members of the athletic squad in the same High School before they entered the service."

"Darrin and Dalzell are going to make it possible for the Navy to wipe us up again this year, too," continued the other cadet plaintively.

"I don't believe they would, if we could put in Mr. Prescott and Holmesy for this year."

"But we can't, Durry."

"No; I know it."

"So what's the use of talking." Nevertheless, there was a lot of talking, and dozens waylaid Greg and tried to induce him to reconsider. But he wouldn't, and that was all there was to it. No one even thought of lifting the ban from Prescott in order to gain either or both of these cadet athletes. West Point cadets are consistent. They will never lift the ban, once they believe it to have been justly laid, just in order to make a better athletic showing. The Academy authorities demand that a team athlete shall stand well in his studies and general discipline; the cadets themselves demand also that the man who carries their athletic colors must conform to cadet ideals of honor. And Prescott, being in Coventry, surely was not to be regarded as a man of honor.

Washington's Birthday had come and passed, and Prescott still lingered in the cadet corps. Indeed, he seemed as determined as ever upon graduating.

There were limits, however, to class patience. It was Anstey who got on the track of the news and brought it to Greg.

"A class meeting is to be called ten days hence," reported the Virginian. "The meeting will be announced at supper formation to-night. It is set well ahead in order to give the fellows plenty of time to think over the subject for discussion."

"That discussion," guessed Holmes, "is to be as to the best means of driving Dick from the corps."

"You've guessed it, suh," replied the Virginian sorrowfully. "Whatever the class feels called upon to do, suh, I reckon it will be something that will break our poor camel's back."

CHAPTER XIII

THE FIGURES IN THE DARK

And Dick?

The reader will hardly need to be told that this spirited young cadet was suffering his unmerited disgrace as keenly as ever.

More keenly, in fact, for every day that the silence continued it seemed to add to the weight of the burden that bound him down.

Yet Greg asked no questions, for he felt that it would be safer not to do so. He had just barely told Prescott of the purpose of the coming class meeting, which the latter cadet had already guessed for himself, however.

"I suppose I'll have a few loyal friends at that meeting?" asked Dick, with a sad smile.

"Just as many friends as ever," asserted Holmes stoutly.

"I'm mighty grateful for that," nodded Dick. "But what I seem to need is more friends than ever."

"We'll find them for you, if there's any way to do it," promised Holmes, and there the talk dropped.

"If the class goes against me again, and harder than before, I'm certain I shall have to see Lieutenant Denton once more and tell him that I can't stand it any longer," Dick told himself.

The class meeting was to be held on a Monday evening. On the night of the Saturday before, when scores of cadets were over at Cullum Hall at a merry "hop," Prescott slipped out of barracks by himself in Greg's absence.

Almost unconsciously Prescott's steps turned in the direction of Trophy Point. In the darkness he stood before Battle Monument, on which are inscribed the names of the West Point graduates who have fallen in battles.

"Will my name ever be there, or have any chance to be there?" wondered Dick, a big lump rising in his throat.

A tear stood in either eye, but he brushed them aside as unworthy of a soldier. Was he ever going to be a soldier, he wondered.

"I don't know that I'm really ready to be killed in battle," thought Dick grimly. "It would be enough to know that my name is to be on the roll of graduates of the Military Academy, and afterwards on the rolls of the Army as an officer who had served with credit wherever he had been placed. But the fates seem against even that much. Hang it all, what was it that Lieutenant Denton said about faith and right, and faith being as much the soldier's duty as honor? I guess he was never placed in just such a fix as mine!"

For, slowly, all of Dick's iron-clad resolution to "stick it out" was wearing away. It was becoming plainer to him, every day, that he could not stay in the Army if he were always to live in Coventry as far as his brother officers were concerned.

"I wonder what the fellows will do at the meeting next Monday night?" Dick pondered, as he turned and strolled back by another road. "If the fellows could only realize how unjust they are without meaning to be! But I can't make them see that. I'll have to resign, of course, but I promised Lieutenant Denton to talk it over with him before doing anything of the sort, and I'll keep my word."

Very absent minded did the young cadet become in the midst of his perplexed musings. He heard the sound of martial music and unconsciously his feet moved in quicker time.

It was as though he were marching, led on by he knew not what.

Straight toward the music he moved, with the tread of a soldier responding to the drums.

Then, at last, when he was almost upon the building, Prescott came to himself and stopped abruptly.

"Cullum Hall!" he muttered, with a harsh laugh. "The night of the cadet hop. My classmates are in there, free-hearted and happy, and taking their lessons in the social graces—-while I am on the outside, the social outcast of the class!"

Yet, as there were no cadets in sight, out at this north end of the handsome building, Prescott presently moved forward, nearer.

"The old, old story of the beggar on the outside! The man on the outside, looking in!" muttered Dick with increasing bitterness. "Yet I may as well look, since there is none to see me or deny me."

Around the north end Dick passed, just as the brilliant music of the Military Academy orchestra was drawing to its close. In his misery the young cadet leaned against the face of the building, behind an angle in the wall.

As he stood there Dick saw the figure of a man flit, by him. The stranger was dressed in citizen's clothes. There was nothing suspicions in that, since there is no law to prevent citizens from visiting the Military Academy. But there was something stealthy about this stranger's movements.

"It is a wonder he didn't see me," mused Dick. "He went by within eight feet of me."

Dick was about to make his presence known by stepping out into sight, when the stranger halted.

"Perhaps it may be as well not to show myself just yet," flashed through Prescott's mind. "If the fellow is up to any mischief probably I can prevent it."

A cold, biting breeze swept up from the Hudson River below. It was chilling in the extreme, here at the top of the bluff, but Dick, in his misery, had been proof against weather.

Not so with the stranger. He stamped his feet and struck his hands against his sides. Then, after some moments, as though angry at some one within Cullum Hall, the stranger wheeled and shook one clenched fist at the windows overhead.

"Whom has that fellow a grouch against?" Dick wondered in spite of himself.

Just an instant later he heard a quick step coming around the north end of the building.

A cadet was coming, beyond a doubt, and very likely to meet this impatient or angry stranger.

Prescott had too much honor to play the eavesdropper. He was just about to step out when the newcomer turned the corner, coming on straight past where Prescott stood in the deep shadow.

The newcomer was a cadet, and that cadet was Mr. Jordan.

"Well, my good fellow, have I kept you waiting long?" demanded Jordan, just the second after he had stepped past Dick without seeing the latter.

"You could a jumped faster," growled the stranger. "With all I know against you, Jordan, it will pay you to nurse my good feeling a little harder."

"Why, what's the matter with you now?" demanded Jordan more seriously.

Somehow, Dick could not pull himself away just then.

"Have you brought me some of that money you owe me?" demanded the stranger gruffly.

"Now, you know I can't, before graduation day," pleaded Jordan whiningly.

"And I know that, when graduation day comes, you'll tell me that every dollar you had in the world had to go into uniforms," snapped the stranger. "I'll tell you what I do know about you, Jordan, my boy. I know that if you don't find the money, turn it over and get back my note, you'll never graduate! Cadets can't borrow money on their notes; it's against the regulations. If it was known that you had borrowed five hundred dollars of me already, and that you were defaulting on principal and interest, too———"

"It wasn't five hundred," broke in Jordan nervously. "It was just two hundred and fifty dollars."

"The note says five hundred," retorted the stranger tersely, with a shrug of his shoulders. And there's interest on it, too. And you haven't paid a dollar. You told me you could get the money from home."

"I——I thought I could, at that," stammered Cadet Jordan. "But I wrote my father, and he said he was near bankruptcy——-"

"Near bankruptcy?" almost screamed the stranger. "You young swindler. You told me your father was a wealthy man!"

"Sh!" begged Jordan tremulously. "Not so loud! Some one will hear you."

"I don't care who hears me," retorted the stranger in an ugly tone. "You've been swindling me right along, it seems. Now, you'll hand me some money to-night, and all of the balance by next Wednesday, or I'll go straight to the superintendent. Then you'll lose your nice little berth here. You putting on airs, and yet you told me how you had rebuked and paid back another cadet for doing the same breezy thing."

Dick, his cheeks burning with the shame of having allowed himself to listen to so much, was on the very point of slipping away around the north end of Cullum Hall. But this last remark gripped him, holding him feverishly to the spot.

"Prescott, I believe you said the fellow's name was," went on the stranger.

"Yes," admitted Jordan. "And I put it all over him in a way that should make anyone else afraid of having me for an enemy!"

Dick's heart gave a great, almost strangling bound. Then it was quiet again, and his ears seemed preternaturally keen.

So sharp was his hearing, in fact, that he heard a sound that did not reach the ears of the other cadet or the latter's companion.

It was someone else coming. With all the stealth in the world Dick now managed to slip around the end of the building and toward the front.

A cadet had stepped out as though seeking a breath of cool air between dances. Dick darted forward on tiptoe until he recognized the oncoming one. It was Douglass, president of the first class.

"Mr. Douglass!" whispered Dick, stopping squarely before his successor in class honors.

Douglass, without looking at his appealing fellow classman, or opening his lips to answer, stepped around Prescott.

But Dick caught his unwilling comrade firmly by the arm.

"Douglass," he whispered, "in the name of justice, listen to me just an instant——a swift instant, too! I think the chance has come to clear me of the load of dislike and contempt with which I am regarded here. This appeal is between man and man! Jordan is around the corner, telling a stranger how he trapped me and got me into disgrace with the class. As a matter of cadet justice and honor, I beg you to go softly to the corner and hear what is being said. Do not let Jordan suspect that you are near. What he is saying will clear me. Go, and go softly, I beg you, as a matter of justice from one man to another!"

All the time that Dick had held his arm Douglass had stood there, not seeking to snatch himself free.

Nor did he utter a word. The class president stood there, like a statue, looking straight past Prescott, as though he did not know that such a being existed anywhere in the world.

Now, with despair tugging at his heart, Prescott released his hold.

Cadet Douglass moved forward again. Dick stood watching his brother cadet with a feeling of despair until he saw that Douglass was moving softly. Dick saw him go quietly around the corner of the building. Now, Dick was at his heels, stealthy as any Indian could have been, until he looked around the corner and saw that Cadet Douglass had slipped into the same shadow that Dick himself had occupied until a moment before.

"Now, if that pair yonder will only go on talking about me for sixty seconds!" thought Dick in a frenzy.

Again he flew toward the front of the building. There was just one other cadet outside—-Durville, the man whom he had been obliged to report for a tremendously grave breach of discipline.

But Dick Prescott's courage was up now. He raced forward, fairly gripping Durville and holding him tight.

"Durville, listen to me for just a moment," begged Dick. "I know you don't like me, but you're a man of honor. Jordan is on the east side of this building, and I believe he is confessing a plot that he put into successful operation against me. Douglass is already there listening. Will you slip there softly, and listen, too? I don't ask this as a matter of friendship, but of honor! Will you go—-and softly?"

Slowly Durville turned and looked into Prescott's eyes. Then he did not speak, but he nodded.

"Thank you, Durville! Be quick—-and stealthy! Let me guide you."

Class President Douglass stood in the shadow. He heard Jordan's own tongue telling the stranger the familiar story of how he, Jordan, had been reported for indolence in the bridge construction work.

"I had to get square," Jordan was continuing, just as Dick piloted Durville within hearing.

"And you think you did it slickly, I suppose?" jeered the stranger.

Though Jordan did not seem to suspect it, the stranger was seeking this information as another blackmailing club to hold over Jordan's head.

"Slick?" queried Jordan, with a sneer. "Well, it wasn't altogether that. There was a good bit of luck in the whole job, too, but Prescott is in Coventry, and there he'll stick, too. He'll be away from here inside of two or three days more."

"How did you manage to do it?" asked the stranger, concealing his anxiety to have Jordan tell the story.

CHAPTER XIV

THE STORY CARRIED ON THE WIND

"Oh, I fixed it all right," insisted Jordan confidently.

He was speaking in a rather low tone, but the breeze carried every word to the ears of the listeners.

"You're talking just to hear yourself talking," sneered the stranger coarsely.

"No; I'm not, Henckley," retorted the cadet.

"What was the trick, then?"

"Don't you wish you knew?" laughed Jordan.

"I don't care much," replied the stranger named Henckley. "But I can't just picture you as doing anything extremely clever. Even if it was luck, as you say, I can't figure how you were smart enough to know how to profit by it. That's why I'm just a bit curious, but no more."

"Why, you see, it happened this way," went on Jordan. "I saw Prescott, that night back into camp, going into the tent of the O.C. I thought that perhaps Prescott was going there in order to say more about the matter that he had reported me for that forenoon. So I moved close and listened. It seemed that some of the plebes had been running the guard nights. Lieutenant Denton asked the fellow Prescott, who is a cadet captain, to keep a watch and stop plebes before they had a chance to get on the other side of the guard line.

"Well, I knew the point at which plebes were in the habit of getting past the guard line, and so did Prescott, I guess. So, a little after taps, I slipped outside the guard near where I judged Prescott would be watching. Then, after I had heard him speak with the cadet sentry I presently stooped low in the bushes and lit a cigar. Then I stood up straight and the glowing end of the cigar showed from where Prescott stood. He did just what a fellow like him feels bound to do, and what I knew he'd do. He hailed me. I acted as though I wanted to get away, then allowed myself to be overhauled. I was reported, of course, and made to pay the penalty. But I was able to make the other fellows in the class believe that Prescott had trailed me, on purpose to rub it into me. That looked like over zeal, backed by a grudge, and the first class swallowed it in fine shape. They gave him the silence, but had not made it permanent Coventry. Then he caught another man, named Durville, for going off the post in 'cit.' clothes, and that settled the case against that fellow Prescott. But it was my trick that made all the rest possible."

"I don't see that that was anything very clever," rejoined Henckley.

"I told you, didn't I," argued Jordan, "that it was as much luck as cleverness."

"What part of it was clever, anyway?" jeered Henckley.

"Why, putting the whole game through, and making the class take it up, yet doing it all so that the trick could never be traced back to me," replied Jordan.

In the shadow, Durville turned briskly, gripping Dick's hand with his own.

Douglass saw. After a bare instant's hesitation the class president also took Prescott's hand, giving it a mighty squeeze.

In the joy of that friendly grasp from his own classmen, Dick Prescott almost felt that all the bitterness of the last few months had been wiped out in a second.

Then Douglass stepped out from the shadow, his face stern and set.

"Perhaps you will want to stop talking, Mr. Jordan," he called. "Your conversation has not been a private one!"

With the strong wind blowing away from Jordan, that cadet heard only a rumble of voices. Both he and Henckley, however, caught sight of the advancing figures.

"Hello! What are you fellows doing here?" demanded the money lender, with blustering indignation.

"I might ask that question of you, fellow, but I won't, for I already know," replied Cadet Douglass, fixing his eyes on the stranger.

"You've been listening to our talk?" demanded Henckley angrily, while Jordan, after his first gasp of dismay, seemed to shrivel back against the wall of Cullum Hall.

"Mr. Jordan," continued the class president, facing the dismayed one in gray uniform, "I don't believe the significance of this meeting has escaped you?"

"No-o-o," wailed Jordan in misery.

"Now, see here, young fellows, don't you go and blab what you've been spying on just now," remonstrated Mr. Henckley, a note of dismay creeping into his tone.

"It can hardly concern you, sir," flashed Cadet Douglass, wheeling upon the money shark. "Yet I suppose it does, too. For now I do not see how Mr. Jordan can hope to remain at the Military Academy. That, I suppose, may possibly affect your security for the money which, I take it, Mr. Jordan has borrowed from you."

"But you won't blab, and have him kicked out?" coaxed Mr. Henckley, his voice now wholly wheedling.

"What the cadets may see fit to do for their own protection is hardly a matter that can be discussed with you, sir," returned Douglass coldly.

"Oh, now see here, there are ways and ways," spoke Henckley in a wheedling tone. "Let's all be friendly."

Before Douglass could guess what was happening the money shark had pressed a hand against the cadet's. With an impatient gesture Douglass shook his own hand free. But something like paper remained in his palm. Douglass held up that hand, and discovered that it held a banknote that Henckley had slipped into Douglass' hand as a bribe.

Cadet Douglass calmly tore that banknote in bits and flung it off on the breeze. The fragments were out of sight in an instant. Then Douglass coolly knocked the money shark down.

"Come along, fellows," spoke the class president quietly, and turned on his heel.

"Confound you, Mr. Fresh, I'll report this to the superintendent," bellowed Henckley.

"Do!" called Douglass in cool contempt over his shoulder.

Douglass, Durville and Prescott tramped together around to the front of Cullum Hall.

There Douglass again paused to hold out his hand, remarking:

"Mr. Prescott, the class meeting is not to be held until Monday evening. All I am privileged to say is that I think what we have overheard tonight will very materially affect the class action. I am very grateful to you, my dear sir, for having called us."

Durville, too, held out his hand in sign that the past grudge was forgotten so far as he was concerned.

Full of a new happiness, Dick trudged back to cadet barracks.

Finding Greg Holmes in, Prescott imparted the wonderful news.

Greg leaped up delightedly, pumphandling his chum's arm and patting him on the back.

"Come out all right?" sputtered Holmes. "Of course it will, and I always knew it would."

Meanwhile Cadet Jordan was surveying Henckley with a look of mingled rage, disgust and consternation.

"Now, you've gone and done it, you bull-necked, toad-brained idiot!" cried the elegant Mr. Jordan.

"Why didn't you pay up like a man, and this would never have happened," growled Henckley, rubbing the spot where Douglass had struck him.

"Pay up like a man?" sneered Jordan. "Well, this affair has one small, good side to it. You've got me run out of the cadet corps, but———"

"Out of the cadet corps?" screamed Henckley. "Then what becomes of what you owe me?"

"That's something you'll have to settle to your own satisfaction," jeered the dismayed cadet. "I can offer you no help."

Jordan turned on his heel, starting to walk away, when Mr. Henckley leaped after him, seizing him by the arm.

"See here———" began the money shark hoarsely.

"Let go of my arm," warned Jordan in a rage, "or I'll hit you harder than Douglass did."

As the money lender shrank back out of Jordan's reach, the cadet strode off swiftly.

Mr. Jordan was in his bed when the subdivision inspector went through the rooms that night.

At morning roll call, however, Jordan did not answer.

An investigation showed that he had gone. All his uniforms and other equipment he had left behind, from which it was judged that Jordan had, in some way, managed to get hold of an outfit of civilian attire.

Jordan had deserted, with a heart full of hate for Dick Prescott, with whom the deserter swore to be "even" before the academic year was out.

CHAPTER XV

THE CLASS MEETING "SIZZLES"

That Sunday, save Greg, none of the cadets addressed Prescott.

Anstey, however, thought up a new way of getting around the "silence." As he passed Dick, the Virginian winked very broadly. Other cadets were quick to catch the idea. Wherever Dick went that Sunday he was greeted with winks.

Monday Dick was in a fever of excitement. For once he fared badly in his marks won in the section rooms.

When evening came around every member of the first class, save Prescott, hurried off to class meeting. For the first time in many months, Greg attended.

As the cadets began to gather, excitement ran high. The room was full of suppressed noise until President Douglass rapped sharply for order.

Then, instantly all became as still as a church.

"Will Mr. Fullerton please take the chair?" asked the class president. "The present presiding officer wishes the privileges of the floor."

Amid more intense silence Fullerton went forward to the chair, while Douglass stepped softly down to the floor.

"Mr. Chairman," called Douglass.

"Mr. Douglass has the floor."

Douglass was already on his feet, of course. He plunged into an accurate narrative of what had happened, and what he had overheard, on Saturday night. He told it all without embellishment or flourish, and wound up by calling attention to Jordan's plain enough desertion from the corps.

Durville then obtained the floor. He corroborated all that the class president had just narrated.

"May I now make a motion, sir?" demanded Durville, turning finally toward the class president.

"Yes," nodded Cadet Douglass.

"Mr. Chairman, I move that the first class, United States Military Academy, remove the Coventry and the silence that have been put upon our comrade, Mr. Richard Prescott. I move that, by class resolution, we express to him our regret for the great though unintentional injustice that has been done Mr. Prescott during these many months."

"I second the motion!" shouted Douglass.

It was carried amid an uproar. If there were any present who did not wish to see Dick thus reinstated, they were wise enough to keep their opinions to themselves.

"Mr. Chairman!" shouted another voice over the hubbub.

"Mr. Mallory," replied the chair.

"I move that Messrs. Holmes and Anstey be appointed a committee of two to go after Mr. Prescott and to bring him here——by force, if necessary."

Amid a good deal of laughter this motion, too, was carried. The two more than willing messengers departed on the run.

"Mr. Chairman!"

"Mr. Douglass."

The class president rose, waving his right hand for utter silence.

Then, slowly and modestly, he said:

"I have greatly enjoyed the honor of being president of this class. But I can no longer take pride in holding this office, for, in common with the rest of you, I realize that I secured the honor through a misapprehension. I therefore tender my resignation as president of the first class."

"No, no, no!" shouted several.

"Thank you, gentlemen," replied Douglass with feeling. "I appreciate it all, but I feel that I have no longer any right to the presidency of the class, and I therefore resign it——renounce it! Gentlemen, comrades, will you do me the favor of accepting my resignation at once?"

"On account of the form in which the request is put," said Durville, as soon as he had secured the chair's recognition, "I move that our president's resignation be accepted in the same good faith in which it is offered."

"Thank you, Durry, old man!" called Douglass in a low voice.

A seconder was promptly obtained. Then Chairman Fullerton put the motion. There were cries of "too bad," but no dissenting votes.

In the meantime Greg and Anstey all but broke down a door in their effort to reach Dick quickly.

"Come on, old chap!" called Greg, pouncing upon his chum. "It's all off! Savvy? We have orders to drag you to class meeting, if force be necessary. Come on the jump!"

"Won't I, though?" cried Dick, seizing his fatigue cap and hurrying on his uniform overcoat.

A smaller mind might have insisted on taking slowly the request from the class that had unintentionally done him such an injustice. But Cadet Prescott was made of broader, nobler stuff. He realized that, without exception, the manly fellows in his class were heartily glad to do him justice, now that they knew how blameless he had been. Dick was as anxious to meet his class as they were to reinstate him.

So he hurried along between the jubilant Holmes and Anstey.

The meeting had just quieted down again by the time that the three cadets entered the room.

But in an instant Halsey was on his feet, regardless of rules of parliamentary procedure.

"Give old ramrod the long corps yell!" he shouted.

With hardly the pause of a second it came, and never had it sounded sweeter, truer, grander than when some hundred powerful young throats sent forth the refrain:

"Rah, rah, ray! Rah, rah, ray! West Point, West Point, Armee Ray, ray, ray! U.S.M.A.!"

"Prescott!"

Dick Prescott's chest began to heave, though he strove to conceal all emotion. It was sweet, indeed, to have all this enthusiasm over him, after he had so long been the innocent outcast of the class.

Tears shone in either eye. Ashamed to raise a hand to brush the moisture away, Dick tried to wink them out of sight.

But Douglass, Durville and the others gave him no time to think. They came crowding about him faster than they could reach him, each with outstretched hand.

Little was said. Soldiers are proverbially silent, preferring deeds to words. So, for nearly ten minutes, the handshaking proceeded. At last Douglass, with a warning nod and several gestures, brought the temporary chairman to his senses.

Rap! rap! rap! rang the gavel on the desk.

"The class will please come to order," called Chairman Fullerton. "Now, gentlemen, is there any further business to come before the class?"

"Mr. Chairman," called Douglass, "I move that we proceed to the election of a class president."

"Second the motion," cried Durville.

The motion was carried with a rush.

"Mr. Chairman!" called the tireless ex-class president.

"Mr. Douglass."

"Mr. Chairman and gentlemen, I am going to make a mistake that has become time honored among public speakers, that of telling you what you already know as well as I do. This is that Mr. Prescott ought never to have been deposed from the class presidency. I move, therefore, sir, that we rectify our stupidity and blindness by making Mr. Prescott once more our president. I beg, sir, to place in nomination for the class presidency the name of Richard Prescott, first class, U.S.M.A."

"I second the nomination, suh!" boomed out the voice of Anstey.

"Other nominations for the class presidency are in order," announced Chairman Fullerton.

Again silence fell.

"Mr. Chairman!"

"Mr. Douglass."

"Since there are no more nominations, I move you, sir, that Mr. Prescott be elected president of this class by acclamation."

"Sir, I second the motion," came from Durville's throat.

There was wild glee as a volley of "ayes" was fired.

"Those of a contrary mind will say 'no,'" requested the chair.

Not a "no" could be heard.

"The chair will now withdraw, after appointing Mr. Douglass, Mr. Durville, Mr. Holmes and Mr. Anstey a committee of honor to escort the new-old class president to the chair."

While the little procession was in motion the windowpanes rattled more than ever, with the long corps yell for Prescott.

The instant his hand touched the gavel, Dick rapped for order.

"Gentlemen of the first class," he said quietly, "I thank you all. Little more need be said. I am sure that mere words cannot express my great happiness at being here. I will not deny that I have felt the injustice of the cloud that has hung over me for the last few months. Anyone of you would have felt it under the same circumstances. But it is past—-forgotten, and I know how happy you all are that the truth has been discovered."

There was a moment's silence. Then Dick asked, as he had so often done before:

"Is there any further business to come before the class meeting?"

Silence.

"A motion to adjourn is in order."

The motion was put, offered and carried. Dick Prescott stepped down from the platform, a man restored to his birthright of esteem from his comrades.

CHAPTER XVI

FINDING THE BASEBALL GAIT

"Morning, old ramrod!"

Never had greeting a sweeter sound than when Dick strolled about in the quadrangle after breakfast the next morning.

Scores who, for months, had looked straight past Prescott when meeting him, now stopped to speak, or else nodded in a friendly manner.

Twenty minutes later, the sections were marching off into the academic building, in the never-ceasing grind of recitations.

"Prescott," declared Durville, during the after-dinner recreation period, "we want you to come around to show what you can do at baseball. We've some good, armor-proof material for the squad, but we need a lot more. And we want Holmesy, too. Bring him around with you, won't you?"

"If he'll come," nodded Dick.

"He must come. But you'll hold yourself ready, anyway, won't you?"

"I'd hate to go in without Greg," replied Dick. "He and I generally work together in anything we attempt."

"That was just the kick Holmesy made when you——when things were different," corrected the captain of the Army nine hastily.

"Well, you see, 'Durry,' we were always chums back in the good old High School days. We always played together, then, in any game, and either of us would feel lonesome now without the other."

"Oh, of course," nodded Durville. "Well, I'll see Holmesy and try to round him up, if you say so."

"I think I can get him to come around," smiled Dick. "But you may be tremendously disappointed in both of us."

"Can you play ball as well as Holmesy?"

"Perhaps; nearly, I guess."

"Then we surely do need you both, for we've seen Holmesy toy with the ball, and we know where he'd rate. Do you think you play baseball at the same gait that you do football, old ramrod?"

"I think it's possible that I do," Dick half admitted slowly.

"Always modest, aren't you?" laughed "Durry" good humoredly. "Somehow, Prescott, it seems almost impossible to think of you heading a charge, or graduating number one in your class. You'd be too much afraid that someone else wanted either honor."

Prescott laughed good humoredly. Then, dropping his voice, he went on very gravely:

"Durry, you've behaved very nicely to me in more ways than one, after that time when I necessarily reported you. Are you sure that you wholly overlooked my act."

"Glad you asked me, Prescott. I've come to realize that you did your full duty, and the only thing you could do as the captain of my company. But I was terribly upset that night. Nothing but a matter of the first importance would ever have driven me to slip into 'cits.' and sneak off the post in that fashion."

"I can quite believe that," nodded Dick.

"Well, it——it was a girl, of course," confessed "Durry."

"You know, cadets have a habit of being interested in girls, and this girl means everything to me. She's up in Newburgh, and was ill. I thought she was more ill than she really was. But I knew that I could hardly get official permission to go and see her, so——so I chanced it and went without leave. I wouldn't have done such a thing under any other circumstances."

"Did the young lady recover?" asked Prescott with deep interest.

"Oh, yes; I dragged her to the hop the other night. She was stepping around the hall with another fellow, for one of the dances, and that was how I came to be out in the air alone. But I'll look for both you and Holmesy at practice this afternoon," ended "Durry," hastening away.

"Go to a diamond try-out?" asked Greg when Dick broached the subject.

"Of course I will, and crazy over the chance. All that has held me back so far, old ramrod, was the fact that you hadn't been invited. But now that has all been changed."

When the diamond squad reported, Lieutenant Lawrence, the head baseball coach, ordered the young men outdoors to the field.

"Come over here, please, Prescott and Holmes," called the coach, who had been conferring in low tones with "Durry."

"What positions do you two feel that you would be at your best in?"

"Why, we have conceit enough, sir, to think that we might make at least a half-way battery," smiled Dick.

"Battery, eh?" repeated Lieutenant Lawrence. "Good enough! Get out and do it. Durville, you're one of the real batsmen. Run out there to the home plate, and see whether Prescott and Holmes can put anything past you."

How good it felt to be in field clothes again! And both Greg and Dick wore on the breasts of their sweaters the Army "A," won by making the football eleven the year before.

Dick fingered the ball carefully while Greg was trotting away to place behind the home plate. Lieutenant Lawrence went more deliberately, but took his place where the umpire would have stood in a game.

"What kind of a ball do you like best, Durry?" asked Prescott, smilingly.

"A medium slow one, close to the end of the stick, about here," replied Durville.

"I'll try to give you something else, then," chuckled Dick.

And give the batsman something else was just what he did.

Crack! Durville swatted the ball. It rose steeply at first, then sailed away gracefully towards the clouds.

"Get a fresh ball!" shouted one member of the training squad. "That leather isn't going to come down again!"

It did, though a scout had to run far afield to pick it up.

Lieutenant Lawrence didn't look exactly disappointed, but he had hoped to see something better than this had been.

Five more Dick pitched in, and of these "Durry" put his mark on three.

"That will be enough to-day, I guess, Mr. Prescott," remarked Lieutenant Lawrence in an even voice.

Poor Dick flushed, but was about to turn away from the pitcher's box when Durville turned to the Army coach.

"If you really don't mind, sir, I'd like to see Prescott throw in a few more. He hasn't held a ball in his hands for a long time, and I think he has only been warming up."

"If you really think it worth while," nodded the lieutenant.

Then, raising his voice:

65

"We'll have you try just a few more, Prescott. Try to astonish everyone!"

Greg, whose face had flushed with mortification, now crouched a bit, sending Dick one of the old-time signals. Holmes was not even sure his chum would remember the signal.

It is doubtful if anyone noticed the return that Dick sent back to show that he understood.

Durville took a good grip on his stick, his alert gaze on the man in the box.

With hardly a trace of flourish Dick let the ball go. On it came, not very swift and straight over the plate. "Durry" himself felt a sinking of the heart that. Dick should let such an easy one leave him.

Yet Durville had his own work to do honestly. He must pound this easy one and drive it as far as he could.

Durville swung and let go. But just as he did so——that ball dropped!

It passed on a level two feet below the swinging stick, and Greg, with a quiet grin, neatly mitted it.

"Good!" muttered Coach Lawrence under his breath. "Got any more like that, Prescott?" he called.

"I think I have a few, sir, when I get my arm warmed up and limbered," Dick admitted.

"Take your time, then. Don't knock your arm out of shape."

Again Greg was signaling, though the signal was so difficult to catch that many of the onlookers wondered if Holmes really had signaled.

Swish——ew——ew——zip!

Again Durville had fanned truly, though nothing but air. The outshoot had seemed to spring lazily around, just out of reach of the end of his stick.

Now, every member of the squad, and all of the spectators were beginning to take keen notice.

"Slowly, Prescott. Take your time between," admonished Lieutenant Lawrence, who knew how easily a pitcher out of training might wrench his muscles and go stale for several days.

Greg had signaled for what had once been one of his chum's best——a modification of the "jump ball" that had cost this young pitcher much hard study and arm-strain.

As Dick stood ready to let go of the ball he seemed inclined to dawdle over it. It wasn't going to be one of his snappiest——any onlooker could judge that, at least, so it seemed.

Even Durville was fooled, though he did not let up much in the way of alertness.

Now the ball came on, with not much speed or steam behind it. Durville took a good look, made some calculation for possible deception, then made his swing with the stick.

Slightly forward Durville had to bend, in order to get low enough to make the crack.

As his bat swished half lazily through the air, Durville "ducked" suddenly, for the upbounding ball had gone so close to his ear as to seem bent on removing some of the skin off that member.

66

Greg, who had been stooping, was up in time to mit the ball.

Then Durville, his face flushing, heard Holmes chuckle.

"One or two more, if you like, sir," called Dick, facing the coach. "But I think, sir, I'd better be in finer trim before I do too much tossing in one afternoon."

"You've done enough, Prescott," cried Lieutenant Lawrence, stepping forward and resting one hand cordially on Dick's shoulder.

"Train with us for a fortnight, and you'll take all the hide off of the Navy's mascot goat."

There was a laugh from the members of the squad who stood within hearing. But, as Dick Prescott and Greg Holmes walked over to the side of the field they were greeted by a cheer from all who had watched their performance.

"I'm very glad you asked for a further trial for Prescott," murmured Lieutenant Lawrence to the captain of the Army nine.

"I thought you would be, sir," Durville replied.

"We have a line-up, after these two men have been trained into shape, that will make one of the strongest Army nines in a generation."

"We'd have tanned the Navy last year, sir," ventured Durville, "if we had known what material we had in Prescott and Holmes, and had been able to get them out."

At cadet mess that evening the talk ran high with joy. West Point was sure it had found its baseball gait!

CHAPTER XVII

READY FOR THE ARMY-NAVY GAME

In between times, in the strenuous hours that followed, Dick found the time, somehow, to write two letters of moment.

One was to his mother, the other to Laura Bentley. In both he told how the last bar to his happiness in the Army had been removed. Yet Dick did not go very deeply into details. He merely explained that the class had discovered, on indisputable evidence, that he had been dealt with unjustly. He made it plain, however, that he was now again in high favor with his class, and that he had even been honored by reelection to the class presidency.

"Greg, you send Dave Darrin a short note for me, will you?" begged Dick, as he toiled away at the missive to Laura. "Old Dave will want only the bare facts; that will be enough for him. He'll cheerfully wait for details until some time when we're all graduated and meet in the service."

Dave Darrin's reply was short, but characteristic:

"Of course dear old Dick came through all right! He's the kind of fellow that always does and always must come through all right——otherwise there'd be no particular use in being manly."

No word came from the missing Jordan. Truth to tell, no one seemed to care, outside of the young man's father. It is rare, indeed, that a cadet deserts, and when he does, unless he has taken government property with him, no effort is made to find him.

By the end of the week, Dick Prescott was the hope of the Army nine, as he had once been of the eleven.

A cadet is always in condition. His daily training keeps him there. So Dick had only to give his arm a little extra work, increasing it some each day.

"Do you think I'm going to be in satisfactory shape, sir?" Dick asked the Army coach Friday afternoon.

"If something doesn't happen to you, Prescott, you're going to be the strongest, speediest pitcher I've ever seen on the Army nine," replied Lieutenant Lawrence.

"Isn't that saying a good deal, sir?"

"Yes; but you're the sort of athlete that one may say a great deal about," replied Lieutenant Lawrence, with a confident smile. "And Mr. Holmes is very nearly as good a man as you are."

"I always thought him fully as good, even better," replied Prescott.

"There isn't much to choose between you," admitted coach. "I wish we could always look for such men on our Army teams."

"You can one of these days, sir."

"When will that day come?"

"It will come, sir, when public-spirited citizens everywhere go in strongly for athletics in the High Schools, as they did in the town where Holmes and I received our earlier training."

The letter from Cadet Prescott's mother came almost by return mail. She had never for a moment lost faith, she wrote, that all would come out right with her boy, and she was heartily glad that her faith had been justified. She was sorry, indeed, for that unfortunate other cadet whose enmity for Dick had been his own undoing in the long run.

It was some days later when Laura's letter reached the now eager pitcher of the Army nine.

Now that letter was cordial enough in every way, and Laura made no secret of her delight and of her pride in her friend.

"Yet there's something lacking here," murmured Prescott uneasily, as he read the letter through once more. "What is it? Laura writes as if she were trying to show more reserve with me than she did once. What is the matter? Has she cooled toward me at just the time when I shall soon be able to offer her my name and my future?"

The thought was torment. Nor, of course, did Dick fail to remember all about that prosperous and agreeable Gridley merchant, Leonard Cameron, who, for upwards of two years, had been one of Miss Bentley's most devoted admirers.

"I suppose he's the kind of fellow who is calculated to please a woman," mused Dick with a sinking at heart. "And Cameron has had the great advantage of being right on the spot all the time. Moreover, he has had his future mapped out for him, while I wasn't assured about my own, and he hasn't been afraid to speak. Great Scott, I must wait until the night of the graduation ball before I can speak and find out how the land lies for me. But is Laura coming to that hop?"

Again Dick ran hastily through the letter. Yet, look as he would, he could find no allusion of Laura's to coming on for the Graduation Hop.

"What an idiot I am!" growled Prescott to himself. "I'm certain I forgot to ask her, in my last letter. If I did, it was solely because I've always been so sure that she'd be on here for graduation week as a matter of course."

After pacing his room for a few moments, Dick sat down and wrote feverishly back to Laura Bentley, asking her if she were coming on for graduation and the hop.

"I've always looked forward to having you here as a matter of course on that great occasion," Dick penned, "so I'm not very certain that I have made the invitation as explicit as I've meant to. But you'll come, won't you, Laura? It would be a poor graduation for me, without your face in the throng, for the others will be strangers to me. Won't you please write promptly and set my mind at ease on this vital point?"

In three days Laura's answer came. Unless unavoidably prevented she would be on hand during a part of graduation week.

"And I certainly want to attend the graduation hop," Laura added, "for it will probably be the only one that I shall ever have a chance to attend."

"Now, what does she mean by that last statement?" pondered Dick, finding new cause for worry. "Does she mean that she expects to cut the Army after this year? Is she really planning to marry that fellow Cameron? Gracious, how time has flown during these hurried years at West Point! For two years past Laura has been fully old enough to wed! What a folly she'd commit in waiting all these years for backward me to get ready to open my lips! Yes; I guess it's going to be Cameron."

Cadet Prescott compressed his lips grimly, but he was soldier enough to be game and face the music.

"I've got to be patient a few weeks more, and take the chances," Dick told himself, as he scurried away to daily ball practice. "With a rival in the field I wouldn't dare, anyway, to trust my fate to a pleading set down on paper. But I'll send Laura a letter once a week now, anyway. She may guess from that, as graduation approaches, that I am sending my thoughts more and more in her direction."

With the bravery of which he was so capable, Dick ceased his worry about his sweetheart as much as he could, and threw his leisure hours heartily into his work in the ball squad.

It will not be possible to describe the games of the season in detail. There were twenty scheduled games in all, though three were called off on account of rain. The Army won twelve out of sixteen games played with college teams. Dick and Greg were the battery in the heaviest nine of the winning games, and in one of the games lost.

Prescott and Holmes had no difficulty in putting up a game that has sent them down in history as being the best Army battery to that date.

But the Navy, that year, had an exceptionally fine team, too, with Dave Darrin and Dalzell for its star battery.

"This is the game we've got to win, fellows," called out Durville earnestly, two days before the Annapolis nine was due at West Point in the latter part of May. "We've done finely this year, better than we had hoped. But, after all, what is it to beat every other college, and then have to go down before the Navy in defeat at the end?"

"Who says we're going down in defeat?" grumbled Greg.

"If you say we're not, you and Prescott, then you can do a lot to hearten us up," continued Durville, with a sharp glance at the star battery pair.

"See here, old ramrod, you know all about that Annapolis battery," broke in Hackett, of the nine. "What about them as ball players? I understand you went to school with Darrin and Dalzell. Do that pair play ball the way they do football?"

"Yes," nodded Dick. "If anything, they play baseball better."

"But you and Holmesy put them out at football. Can't you do it on the diamond, too?" insisted Hackett.

"I hope so, but Greg and I will feel a lot more like bragging, possibly, after we've played the game through. There isn't much brag about us now, eh, Greg?"

"Not much," confessed Greg. "And you fellows want to remember that old ramrod and I are to play only two out of the nine positions. Don't depend on us to play the whole game for the Army."

"Of course not," agreed Hackett, perhaps a bit tartly. "But if the other seven of us were wonders we'd stand no show unless we had a battery that can do up these awful ogres of the Navy nine."

"Oh, you're better than the Navy battery, aren't you, old ramrod?" demanded Beckwith.

"No, we're not," replied Dick slowly, thoughtfully.

"Don't tell us that the salt-water catcher and pitcher are ahead of you two!" protested Durville with new anxiety.

"If either crowd is better, they're likely to be It," murmured Dick.

Thereupon all in the dressing room wheeled to take a look at Greg.
But young Holmes nodded his head in confirmation.

"Don't talk that way," pleaded Beckwith.

"You'll have us all scared cold before we touch foot to the field day after to-morrow."

"Just what I said," grumbled Greg. "Some of the fellows on the Army nine expect two men who are not above the average to win the whole game."

From all private and newspaper accounts many of the West Point fans were inclined to the belief that the Navy outpointed the Army in the matter of battery. It had been so the year before when, as readers of "*Dave Darrin's Third Year At Annapolis*" will recall, the Navy had succeeded in carrying the game away with neatness and despatch.

"You young men have simply got to hustle and keep cool. That's all you can do," urged Lieutenant Lawrence. "We haven't had so good a nine in years. Whatever you do, don't lie down at the last moment, and give up to the Navy the only game of the year that is really worth winning."

Then came two hard afternoons of practice. Every onlooker watched Dick and Greg closely, anxious to make sure that neither young man was going stale.

With each added hour it must be confessed that anxiety at West Point rose another notch.

Then came the day of the game. Even the tireless and merciless instructors over in the Academic Building eased up a bit on the cadets that day, if ever the instructors did such a thing.

70

The Annapolis nine arrived before one o'clock and was promptly taken to dinner.

All that forenoon, the factions had been gathering.

Most of the visitors, to be sure, came to "root" for the Army, though there were not wanting several good-sized crowds that came to cheer and urge the Navy young men on to victory.

By noon there were three thousand outsiders on the West Point reservation. Afternoon trains, stages and automobiles brought crowds after that. By three o'clock everyone that expected to see the game had arrived. There were now nine thousand people on the grandstands and along the sides.

"Nine?" repeated Durville in the dressing room, when the word was brought to him. "Five thousand used to be about the usual crowd, I believe. Old ramrod, you and Holmesy are surely responsible for the other four thousand. Darrin and Dalzell can't have done it all, for the Navy always travels light on baggage when headed this way. Yes, you and Holmesy have dragged the crowd in."

"Quit your joshing," muttered Greg, who was bending over his shoe laces.

"Yes; cut it. We can stand it better after the game," laughed Dick.

"Get your men out in five minutes more, Durville," called Lieutenant Lawrence, looking in. "The Navy fellows have been on the field ten minutes already. You want to limber up your men a bit before game is called."

Already the sound had reached dressing quarters of the visiting fans cheering for the Navy.

In three minutes more the cheering ascended with four times as much volume, for now Durville marched the picked Army nine on to the field, and the fans on the stands caught sight of these trim young soldiers.

"I've got a hunch you'll do it for us to-day," whispered Beckwith in Prescott's ear.

"Look out. A little hunch is a dangerous thing," retorted Dick, with a grim smile.

CHAPTER XVIII

DAN DALZELL'S CRABTOWN GRIN

Six minutes later, the umpire called the captains to the home plate for the toss.

"There they are——the same old chums!" cried Dick, hitting Greg a nudge.

Darrin and Dalzell, of the Navy nine, had been trying to catch the eyes of the Army battery.

Now the four old chums raced together to a point midway between pitcher's box and home plate. There they met and clasped each others' hands.

"The same old pair, I know!" cried Dave Darrin heartily.

"And we think as much of you two as ever, even if you are in the poor old Army," grinned Dan. "We've come all the way up from Crabtown to teach you how to play ball. The knowledge will probably prove useful to you some day."

"Why, Dick," protested Holmes in mock astonishment, "these cabin boys seem to think they can really play ball!"

"And all I'm afraid of is that they can," laughed Dick.

"Can't we, though——just!" mocked Dan, dancing a brief little step. "Wait until you take a stick to our work, and then see where you'll live!"

"Cut it, Danny, little lion-fighter, cut it!" warned Dave Darrin, with quiet good nature. "You know what they tell us all the time, down at Crabtown——that 'brag never scuttled a fighting ship yet.'

"Dave, you don't expect Danny to believe that, do you?" asked Greg, grinning hard. "Danny never went into anything that he didn't try to win by scaring the other side cold. If our instructors here know what they're talking about, hot air isn't necessarily fatal to the enemy."

"I can tell you one thing, anyway," chipped in Dan, while the other three grinned indulgently at him.

"Yes; you have it straight that this is to be the Army's game," mocked Greg. "But we knew that before we saw you to-day."

"There goes our joy-killer," grunted Prescott, as the umpire's shrill whistle sounded in. "Dave, we'll be in the Navy's dressing room just as soon as——"

"Just as soon as this cruel war is over," hummed Dan.

The toss having been won by the Navy, the captain of that nine had chosen to go to bat.

Now the players on both sides were scattering swiftly to their posts.

Dick took but a bound or two back to the box, just as the umpire broke the package around the new ball and tossed it to the Army pitcher.

"Play ball!"

It was on, with a rush, and a cheer, led by some eight measures of music from the Military Academy Band, which had been quiet for a few minutes.

Then the cheer settled down, for Prescott found himself facing Dan Dalzell at the bat, with Darrin on deck.

"Wipe 'em!" signaled Greg's antics.

Now, to "wipe" Dalzell, who had known everyone of Dick's old curves and tricks in former days, did not look like a promising task, for Dalzell, in addition to his special knowledge about this pitcher, was an expert with the bat. But there might be a chance to put Dan on the mourner's bench. If Dalzell succeeded in picking up even a single from Dick's starting delivery, then Dave could be all but depended upon to push his Navy chum a bag or two further around the course.

"If I can twist Dan all up, it may serve to rattle Dave, too," thought the Army pitcher like a flash.

Dalzell poised the bat, and stood swinging it gently, with an expectant grin that, had it been a school audience, would have made the youngsters on the bleachers yell:

"Get your face closed tight, Danny! That grin hides the stick!"

Dalzell had often had that hurled at him in the old days, but he did not have to dread it now. But Prescott knew that old broad grin. It was Dalzell's favorite "rattler" for the balltosser.

"I think I know the scheme for getting the hair off your goat," mused Prescott, as he sent in his first.

"Ball one!" called the umpire.

Dan's grin broadened.

"Ball two!"

Dalzell knew he had the Army pitcher going now, and didn't take the trouble to reach for the ball.

"Strike one!"

That took some of the starch out of the Navy batsman, who suddenly realized that this twirler for the Army was up to old tricks.

"Strike two!"

Dan was sure he had that one, and he missed it only by an inch.

Gone, now, was the grin on Dalzell's face. A frown gathered between his eyes as he took harder hold of the stick and waited.

Nor did Prescott keep him long waiting. The ball came in, and Dan gauged it fairly well. Yet he fanned for the third time.

"Batsman out!"

Dan hesitated an almost imperceptible instant at the plate. Swift as lightning he made a wry little mouth at Prescott. It nearly broke Dick up with laughter as Dalzell stalked moodily to the bench and Dave stepped forward.

In fact, the Army pitcher choked and shook so that Durville called to him in a quiet, anxious voice from shortstop's beat:

"Anything wrong, ramrod?"

None of the spectators heard this, but most of them saw Dick's short, vigorous shake of the head as he palmed the ball.

Then he let it go, for Darrin was waiting, and in grand old Dave's eyes flashed the resolve to retrieve what had just been taken from the Navy.

"Darry can't lose, anyway. He'll take the conceit out of these Army hikers," predicted some of the knowing ones among the Navy fans.

"Ball one!"

Though not sure, Dave had expected this, and did not try keenly for Dick's first delivery, which, as he knew of old, was seldom of this pitcher's best.

Then came what looked like a high ball. Of old, this had been the poorest sort for Darrin to bit, and Dick seemed to remember it. But Darrin had changed with the years, and he felt a swift little jolt of amusement as he swung for that high one.

Just about three feet away from the plate, however, that ball took a most unexpected drop, and passed on fully eighteen inches under the swing of Darrin's stick.

"Strike one!"

At the next Darrin's judgment forbade him to offer, but the umpire judged it a fair ball, and called:

"Strike two!"

Dalzell, on the bench, was leaning forward now, his chin plunged in between his hands.

"Dick Prescott hasn't lost any of his knack for surprises," muttered Danny. "And if we, who know his old tricks, can't fathom him at all, what are the other seven of us going to do?"

As the ball arched slowly back into Dick's hands, Dalzell, in his anxiety, found himself leaping to his feet.

And now Prescott pitched, in answer to Greg's signal, what looked like a coming jump ball.

Dave Darrin knew that throw, and was ready. In another instant he could have dropped with chagrin, for the ball, after all, was another "drop," and Greg Holmes had mitted it for the Army in tune to the umpire's:

"Strike three-out! Two out!"

"David, little giant, your hand!" begged Dalzell, in a fiery whisper as his chum reached the bench.

"What's up?" asked Darrin half suspiciously.

"Agree with me, now——make deep and loud the solemn vow that we'll use Dick and Greg just as they've treated us!"

"We will, if we can," nodded Darrin, more serious than his chum. "But I always try to tell you, Danny boy, that it's best not to do your bragging until after you've scuttled your ship."

Just as Dave had stepped away from the plate, Hutchins, the little first baseman of the Navy, had bounded forward.

Hutchins was wholly cool, and had keen eye for batting. He hoped, despite what he had heard of Prescott's cleverness, to send Navy spirits booming by at least a two-bagger.

"Strike one!"

Prescott had not wasted any moments, this time, and Hutchins was caught unawares. The little first baseman flushed and a steely look came into his eyes.

At the next one he struck, but it came across the plate as an out-shoot that was just too far out for Hutchins's reach. Had he not offered it would have been a "called ball."

With two strikes called against him, and nothing moving, Hutchins felt the ooze coming out of his neck and forehead. The Navy had been playing grand ball that spring. It would never do to let the Army get too easy a start.

But Dick poised, twirled and let go. It was a straight-away, honest and fair ball that he sent. To be sure there was a trace of in-shoot about it that made Hutchins misjudge it so that, in the next instant, the passionless umpire sounded the monotonous solo:

"Strike three——and out. Side out!"

From the Navy seats dead calm, but from the band came a blare of brass and a clash of drums and cymbals as the cheering started.

In an instant, out of all the hubbub, came the long corps yell from the cadets, ending with:

"Prescott! Holmes!"

Sweet music, indeed, to the Army battery. But Greg heard it on the wing, so to speak, for at the changing of the sides he had hastened forward, so as to pass Dan Dalzell:

"Danny boy, after the game, I want you to do something big for me," whispered Cadet Holmes.

"Surely," murmured Dalzell. "What shall it be?"

"I think I know how you get that grin of yours, that conquering grin on your face, but I wish you'd show me how you make it stick!"

"Call you out for that some day," hissed Dalzell, as, with heightened color, he made his way to catcher's post of duty behind the plate.

Dave Darrin received the ball, and handled it, after the ways of his kind, for a few seconds, to detect any irregularities there might be to its surface or any flaws in its roundness.

"Play ball!" called the umpire.

With Beckwith holding the stick, and Durville on deck, Dick had time to do what he was most anxious to do——to make a study of any new things that Darrin might have learned.

Dave appeared to be fully warmed at the start. "Strike one!" called the umpire, though Beckwith had not dared offer.

Then:

"Strike two!"

Dick began to see light. Dave was in fine form, and was sending them in with such terrific speed that it was barely possible to gauge them. That style of pitching carried big hopes for a Navy victory!

CHAPTER XIX

WHEN THE ARMY FANS WINCED

As Darrin sent in the third ball Beckwith made a desperate sweep for it. It was not to be his, however.

"Three strikes! Striker out!"

That broad grin had come back to Dan Dalzell's face, as he held up the neatly mitted ball for an instant, then hurled it lazily back to Dave Darrin.

Now, Durville came to bat, and the captain of the Army nine was an accurate and hard hitter.

"Ball one!"

"Strike one!"

"Strike two!"

"Ball two!"

Then came a slight swish of willow against leather. Durville had at last succeeded in just touching the ball. But it was a foul hit, and that was all. Dan, however, was not out at the side in time to pick that foul into his own mitten.

Durville, his face somewhat pale and teeth clenched, stood ready for his last chance. It came, in one of Darrin's trickiest throws. It was no use, after all. Durville missed, and Dalzell didn't.

"Strike three——striker out!"

"Prescott, you know that Navy fellow! Go after him——hammer him all the way down the river!" groaned Durville in a low voice as Dick came forward.

Dan's quick ears heard, however, and his grin broadened. Well enough Dalzell knew that Darrin had a lot of box tricks secreted that would fool even a Prescott.

But Dick was not to be rattled, at any rate. He picked up the bat, "hefted" it briefly, then stepped up beside the plate, ready in a few seconds after Durville had gone disconsolately back to the bench.

"I won't try to decipher Dave's deliveries; I'll judge them by what they look like after the ball has started," swiftly decided Prescott.

"Ball one!"

"Ball two!"

"Strike one!"

"Strike two!"

"Crack!"

So fast did Prescott start when that fly popped, that he was nearly half way to first base when he dropped his bat. It was only a fly out to right field, but it was a swift one, and it struck turf before the Navy fielder could hoof it to the spot. He caught it up, whirled, and drove straight to first, but Prescott's toe had struck the bag a fraction of a second before.

"Runner safe at first!" called the umpire quietly. Then the ball went back to Dave, who now had a double task of alertness, for Holmes held the bat at the plate, while Prescott was trying to steal second. Well did Dave Darrin know the trickiness of both these Army players!

Greg, too, was cool, though a good deal apprehensive. With him the call stood at balls three and strikes two when Greg thought he saw his real chance.

Swat! Greg struck with all his strength, and at the sound, a cheer rose from the seats of the Army fans. But the ball was lower than Greg had calculated, and after all his assault on the leather had resulted only in a bunt.

Navy's pitcher took a few swift steps, then bent, straightened up and sent the ball driving to first.

"Runner out at first!"

Then indeed a wail went up. What did it matter that Prescott had reached second? Greg's disaster had put the side out. And now the Navy came back to bat. In this half of the second, three hits were taken out of Prescott's delivery, and at one time there were two sailors on bases. Then the Navy went out to grass and the Army marched in for a trial. This time, however, the Army had neither Durville, Prescott nor Holmes at the plate, and with these three best batters on the bench, Dave had the satisfaction of striking the soldiers out in one, two, three.

In the third inning neither side scored. Then, in the fourth, with two sailors out when he came to bat, Dalzell exploded a two-bagger that brought the Navy to its feet on the benches, cheering and hat-waving. By the time that Dan's flying feet had kicked the first bag on the course Dave Darrin was holding the willow and standing calmly by the plate, watching.

Two of Dick's offers, Dave let go by without heeding, one ball and one strike being called. But Dave, though he looked sleepy, was wholly alert. At the third offer he drove a straight, neat little bunt that was left for the Army's second baseman. That baseman had it in season to drive to Lanton, at Army first base. But Dave had hit the bag first, and was safe, while Dan Dalzell was making pleased faces over at third.

Now, a member of the Navy team slipped over to that side of the diamond to coach Dan on his home-running. In addition to pitching, Dick had to watch first and third bases, in which situation Dave Darrin, with great impudence and coolness, stole second in between two throws.

On the faces of the Army fans, by this time, anxiety was written in large letters. They had heard much about the Navy battery, but not of its base-running qualities.

It was little Hutchins now again at the bat. His last time there he had been struck out without trouble.

"But, it never does to be too positive that a fellow is a duffer," mused Prescott grimly, as he gripped the leather.

Just when little Hutchins seemed on the point of going to pieces he misjudged one of Dick's puts so completely that he struck it, by accident, a fearful crack. A cloud of dust marked the limits of the diamond, while the air was filled with yells and howls. When the dust cleared and the howls had subsided it was found that Dalzell had loped in across the home plate, Darrin had come along more swiftly and was in, while Hutchins touched the second base an instant after the ball had nestled in Greg Holmes's Army mitt.

It mattered little that Earl, who came next to bat, struck out.

The Navy had pulled in two runs——the only runs scored so far!

In the other half the Army nine secured nothing.

In the fifth neither team scored. In the sixth the Navy scored one more run. In the sixth Lanton, of the Army, got home with a single run.

Thus, at the beginning of the seventh, the score stood at three to one with the grin on the Naval face.

During the seventh inning nothing was scored. Now, the sailor boys came to bat for the first half of the eighth, with a din of Navy yells on the air. West Point's men came back with a sturdy assortment of good old Military Academy yells, but the life was gone out. The Army was proud of such men as Durville, Prescott, Holmes, but admitted silently that Darrin and Dalzell appeared to belong to a slightly better class of ball.

"It's our fault, too," muttered the Army coach, Lieutenant Lawrence, to a couple of brother officers. "Darrin and Dalzell have been training with the Navy nine for two years, while Prescott and Holmes came in late this season. Even if they wouldn't play last year, these two men of ours should have reported for the very first day's work last February."

"Prescott couldn't do it," remarked Lieutenant Denton, who had just joined the group.

"Why not, Denton?" asked Lieutenant Lawrence.

"He was in Coventry."

"Pshaw!"

"Didn't you know that?" asked Denton.

"Not a word of it, though Durville once hinted to me that there was some sort of reason why Prescott couldn't come in."

"There was——the Coventry," Denton replied. "But that trouble blew over when the first classmen found themselves wrong in something of which Jordan had accused Prescott."

"Humph!" growled Lieutenant Lawrence, in keen displeasure. "Then, if we lose to-day, the first class can blame itself!"

"You think our battery pair better than the Navy's, then?" asked
Lieutenant Denton.

"Our men would have been better, by a shade, anyway, had they been as long
in training. But as it is———"

"As it is," supplied another officer in the group, "we are wiped off the slate by
the Navy, this year, and no one can know it better than we do ourselves."

Just as the fortunes of war would have it, Dan Dalzell again stood by the plate
at the beginning of the eighth.

"Wipe off that smile, Danny boy," called Darrin softly.

But Dan only shook his head with a deepening grin which seemed to declare
that he found the Navy situation all to the good.

In fact, Dalzell felt such a friendly contempt for poor old Dick's form by this
time, that he cheerily offered at Dick's first.

Crack! That ball arched up for right field, and Dan, hurling his bat, started to
make tracks and time. Beckwith, however, was out in right field, and knew what
was expected of him. He ran in under that dropping ball, held out his hands and
gathered it in.

Dick smiled quietly, almost imperceptibly, while Dan strolled mournfully back
to the bench. Then Prescott turned, bent on annihilating his good old friend
Darrin, if possible. In great disgust, Dave struck out. The look on the Navy fan's
faces could be interpreted only as saying:

"Oh, well, we don't need runs, anyway!"

But when Hutchins struck out——one, two, three!——after as many offers, Navy
faces began to look more grave.

"Hold 'em down, Navy——hold 'em down!" rang the appeal from Navy seats
when the Army went to bat in the eighth.

Dick was first at bat now, with Greg on deck. As Prescott swung the willow
and eyed Darrin, there was "blood" in the Army pitcher's eyes.

Then Darrin gave a sudden gasp, for, at his first delivery, Dick sized up the
ball, located it, and punched it. That ball dropped in center field just as Dick was
turning the first bag. It sped on, but Dick turned back from too big a risk.

But he looked at Greg, waiting idly at bat, and Holmes caught the full meaning
of that appealing look.

"It's now or never," growled Greg between his teeth. "It's seldom any good to
depend at all on the ninth inning."

Darrin, with a full knowledge of what was threatened to the Navy by the
present situation, tried his best to rattle Greg. And one strike was called on
Holmesy, but the second strike he called himself by some loud talk of bat
against leather. Then, while the ball sped into right field, Greg ran after it,
stopping, however, at first bag, while Prescott sprinted down to second bag,
kicked it slightly, and came back to it.

It was up to Lanton, of the Army, now! In this crisis the Army first baseman
either lacked true diamond nerve, or else he could not see Darrin's curves well,
for Lanton took the call of two strikes before he was awarded called balls
enough to permit him to lope contentedly away to first. This advanced both Dick
and Greg.

Bases full——no outs! Three runs needed!

This was the throbbing situation that confronted Cadet Carter as he picked up an Army bat and stood by the plate, facing the "wicked" and well-nigh invincible Darrin of the Navy!

CHAPTER XX

THE VIVID FINISH OF THE GAME

On both sides of the field, every one was standing on seats.

Even the cadets had risen to their feet, every man's eye turned on the diamond, while the cadet cheer-master danced up and down, ready to spring the yell of triumph if only Carter and the player on deck could give the chance.

Lieutenant Lawrence wiped his perspiring face and neck. The coach probably suffered more than any other man on the field. It was his work that had prepared for this supreme game of the whole diamond season!

Over at third base Cadet Prescott danced cautiously away, yet every now and then stole nearly back. Dick was never going to lose a scored run through carelessness.

"Now, good old Carter, can't you?" groaned Durville, as the Army batsman went forward to the plate.

"Durry, I'll come home with my shield, or on it," muttered Carter, with set teeth and white lips as he went to pick up the bat that he was to swing.

Carter was not one of the best stick men of the Army baseball outfit, but there is sometimes such a thing as batting luck. For this, Carter prayed under his breath.

Darrin, of course, was determined to baffle this strong-hope man of West Point. He sent in one of his craftiest outshoots. For a wonder, Carter guessed it, and reached out for it——but missed.

"Strike two!" followed almost immediately from the placid's umpire's lips.

Everyone who hoped for the Army was trembling now.

Dan Dalzell did some urgent signaling. In response, Darrin took an extra hard twist around the leather, unwound, unbent and let go.

Crack! Batter's luck, and nothing else!

"Carter, Carter, Carter!" broke loose from the mouths of half a thousand gray-clad cadets, and the late anxious batter was sprinting for all there was in him.

Just to right of center field, and past, went the ball——a good old two-bagger for any player that could run.

From third Dick came in at a good jog, but he did not exert himself.
He had seen how long it must take to get the ball in circulation.

As for Holmes, he hit a faster pace. He turned on steam, just barely touching third as he turned with no thought of letting up this side of the home plate.

Lanton made third——he had to, for Carter was bent on kicking the second bag in time.

Had there been another full second to spare Carter would have made it. But Navy center field judged that it would be far easier to put Carter out than to play that trick on Lanton, since the latter had but ninety feet to run, anyway.

So Carter was out, but Lanton was hanging at third, crazy with eagerness to get in.

It all hung on Lanton now. If he got across the home plate in time enough it would give the Army the lead by one run. At this moment the score was tied—- three to three!

"Get out there and coach Lantin, old ramrod," begged "Durry," and Dick was off, outside of the foul line, his eye on Dave Darrin and on every other living figure of the Navy nine.

It was Holden up, now, and, though the cadets on the grandstand looked at Carter briefly, with praise in their eyes for his two-bagger that had meant two runs, the eyes of the young men in gray swiftly roved over by the plate, to keep full track of Holden's performance.

But Holden struck out, and Army hopes sank. Tyrrell came in to the plate, and on him hung the last hope. If he failed, Army fans would be near despair.

Dave Darrin was beginning to feel the hot pace a bit, for in this inning he had exerted himself more than in any preceding one. However, that was all between Darrin and himself. Not another player on the field guessed how glad Dave would be for the end of the game. Yet he steeled himself, and sent in swift, elusive ones for Tyrrell to hit.

Swat! Tyrrell landed a blow against the leather, at the last chance that he had at it. It was a bunt, but Navy's shortstop simply couldn't reach it in time to pick it up without the slightest fumble. That delay brought Lanton home and over the plate.

How the plain resounded with cheers! For now the Army led by a single run, and Tyrrell was safe at first.

Jackson up, with Beckwith on deck. There was hope of further scoring.

Yet no keen disappointment was felt when Jackson struck out.

In from pasture trooped the Navy men, eager to retrieve all in the ninth.

"Fit to stay in the box, old ramrod?" anxiously asked "Durry," as the nines changed.

"Surely," nodded Dick.

"Don't stick it out, unless you know you can do the trick," insisted the Army captain earnestly.

"I'm just in feather!" smiled Dick.

Greg, too, had been a bit anxious; but when the first ball over the plate stung his one unmitted hand, Holmes concluded that Prescott did not need to be helped out of the box just at that time.

Then followed something which came so fast that the spectators all but rubbed their eyes.

One after another Dick Prescott struck out three Navy batsmen.

Greg Holmes made this splendid work perfect by not letting anything pass him.

That wound up the game, for Navy had not scored in the ninth, and the rules forbade the Army nine to go again to bat to increase a score that already stood at four to three.

Instantly the Academy band broke loose. Yet above it all dinned the cheers of the greater part of the nine thousand spectators present.

As soon as the band stopped the corps yell rose, with the names of Durville, Prescott and Holmes, and of Carter whose batting luck had played such a part in the eighth.

But, by the time that the corps yell rose the Army nine was nearly off the field.

"Listen to the good noise, old ramrod," glowed Greg.

"It's the last time we'll ever hear the corps yell for any work we do in West Point athletics," went on Greg mournfully.

"I know it," sighed Dick. "If we ever hear cheers for us again, we'll have to win the noise by a gallant charge, or something like that."

"In the Army," replied Greg, choking somewhat.

"Yes; in the good old Army," went on Dick, his eyes kindling. "I don't feel any uneasiness about getting through the final exams. now. We're as good as second lieutenants already, Holmesy!"

While thus chatting, however, the two chums were keeping pace with their comrades of the nine. The nine from Annapolis moved in a compact group a little ahead down the road.

Just before the Army ball-tossers reached the dressing quarters, Lieutenant Lawrence, their coach, hastened ahead of them, meeting them in the doorway.

"The best nine we've had in a long number of years, gentlemen," glowed coach, as he shook the hand of each in passing. "Thank you all for your splendid, hard work!"

Thanks like that was sweet music, after all. But Dick raced to dressing quarters full of but one thing.

"Quick, Holmesy! We don't know how soon the Navy team may have to run down the road to a train."

"Aren't they going to have supper at the mess?" demanded Greg, as he stripped.

"I don't know; I'm afraid not."

Dick and Greg were the first of the Army nine to be dressed in their fatigue uniforms. Immediately they made a quick break for the Navy quarters.

"It looks almost cheeky to throw ourselves in on the other fellows," muttered Greg dubiously. "Some of the middies will think we've come in on purpose to see how they take their beating."

"They didn't get a bad enough beating to need to feel ashamed," replied Dick. "And we won't say a word about the game, anyway."

"May we come in?" called Prescott, knocking on the door of the middies' quarters.

"Who's there?" called a voice. Then the Navy coach, in uniform, opened the door.

"Oh, come in, gentlemen," called the coach, holding out his hand. "And let me congratulate you, Prescott and Holmes, on the very fine game that you two had a star part in putting up for the nine from Crabtown."

"Thank you, sir," Dick replied. "But we didn't call on that account. There are two old chums of ours here, sir, that we're looking for."

"See anything of them anywhere?" smiled Dave Darrin, stepping forward, minus his blouse and holding out both hands.

Dick and Greg pounced upon Dave. Then Dan struggled into another article of clothing and ran forward from the rear of the room.

"How soon do you go?" asked Dick eagerly.

"The 6.14 train to New York," replied Dave.

"Oh, then you're not going to have supper at cadet mess?" asked Greg in a tone of deep disappointment.

"No," answered Dan Dalzell. "It would get us through too late. We dine in New York on arrival."

"Hurry up and get dressed," Dick urged. Then, turning to the coach, he inquired:

"May we keep Darrin and Dalzell with us, sir, until your train leaves?"

"No reason on earth why you shouldn't," nodded the Navy coach.

So Dave and Dan were dressed in a trice, it seemed, though with the care that a cadet or midshipman must always display in the set of his immaculate uniform.

Dick seized Dave by the elbow, marching him forth, while Greg piloted Dan.

"Great game for you———" began Dan, as soon as the quartette of old chums were outside.

"Send all that kind of talk by the baggage train," ordered Cadet Holmes. "What we want to talk about are the dear old personal affairs."

"You youngsters are through here, after not so many more days, aren't you?" began Darrin.

"Yes; and so are you, down at Annapolis," replied Prescott.

"Not quite," rejoined Dave gravely. "There's this difference. In a few days you'll be through here, and will proceed to your homes. Then, within the next few days, you'll both receive your commissions as second lieutenants in the Army, and will be ordered to your regiments. You're officers for all time to come! We of the first class at Annapolis will receive our diplomas, surely. But what beyond that? While you become officers at once, we have to start on the two years' cruise, and we're still midshipmen. After two years at sea, we have to come back and take another exam. If we pass that one, then we'll be ensigns— officers at last. But if we fail in the exam, two years hence then we're dropped from the service. After we've gone through our whole course at Annapolis we still have to guess, for two years, whether we're going to be reckoned smart enough to be entitled to serve the United States as officers. I can't feel, Dick, that we of Annapolis, get a square deal."

"It doesn't sound like it," Prescott, after a moment, admitted. "Still, you can do nothing about it. And you knew the game when you went to Annapolis."

"Yes, I knew all this four years ago," Darrin admitted. "Still, the four years haven't made the deal look any more fair than it did four years ago. However, Dick, hang all kickers and sea-lawyers! Isn't it grand, anyway, to feel that you're in your country's uniform, and that all your active life is to be spent under the good old flag—always working for it, fighting for it if need be!"

"Then you still love the service?" asked Dick, turning glowing eyes upon his Annapolis chum.

"Love it?" cried Dave. "The word isn't strong enough!"

"Are you engaged, old fellow?" asked Greg of Dan Dalzell.

"Kind of half way," grinned Dan. "That is, I'm willing, but the girl can't seem to make up her mind. And you?"

"I've been engaged nine times in all," sighed Greg. Yet each and every one of the girls soon felt impelled to ask me to call it off."

"Any show just at present?" persisted Dalzell.

"Why, strange to say," laughed Greg, "I'm fancy free at the present moment."

"How did the old affair ever come out between Dick and Laura Bentley?" asked Dan curiously.

"Why, the strange part of it is, I don't believe there ever has been any formal affair between Dick and Laura," Greg went on. "That is, no real understanding between them. And now———"

"Yes?" urged Dan.

"A merchant over in Gridley, a rather decent chap, too, has been making up to Laura pretty briskly, I hear by way of home news," Greg continued.

"Does the yardstick general win out?" demanded Dan.

"From all the news, I'm half afraid he does."

"How does Dick take that?" Dan was eager to know.

"I can't tell you," Greg responded solemnly, "for I have never ventured on that topic with old ramrod. But if he loses out with Laura, I feel it in my bones that he'll take it mighty hard."

"Poor old Dick!" sighed Dan, loyal to the old days. "Somehow, I can't quite get it through my head that it's at all right for anyone to withhold from Dick Prescott anything he really wants."

Greg sighed too.

"Any idea what arm of the service you're going to choose?" asked Dan presently.

"I believe I'll do better to wait and see what my class standing is at graduation," laughed Greg. "That is the thing that settles how much choice I'm to have in the matter of arm of the service."

"Any liking for heavy artillery?" asked Dan.

"Not a whit. Cavalry or infantry for mine."

"Not the engineers?"

"Only the honor men of the class can get into the engineers," grunted Greg. "Neither Dick nor I stand any show to be honor men. We feel lucky enough to get through the course and graduate at all."

Dick and Dave, too, were talking earnestly about the future, though now and then a word was dropped about the good old past, as described in the *High School Boys' Series.*

Ten minutes before the train time two chums in Army gray and two in Navy blue reached the platform of the railway station. The other middies were there ahead of them. In the time that was left Dick and Greg were hastily introduced to the other middies. A few jolly words there were, but the other members of the Army nine and still other cadets were on hand, and so the talk was general.

Amid noisy, heartfelt cheering the middy delegation climbed aboard the incoming train. Amid more cheers their train bore them away and then some sixty West Point cadets climbed the long, steep road, next hastening on to be in time for supper formation.

For the members of the first class West Point athletics had now become a matter of history only!

CHAPTER XXI

A CLOUD ON DICK'S HORIZON

Final exams. were passed! Not a member of the first class had "fessed" himself down and out, so all were to be graduated.

The Board of Visitors——a committee of United States Senators and Representatives appointed by the President from among the members of the National Congress, arrived.

A detachment of cavalry and another of field artillery, both from the Regular Army, rode to the railway station to aid in the reception of the Board.

Also the entire Corps of Cadets, two battalions of them, in spick and span full-dress uniform, and with all metal accoutrements glistening, in the sun, stood drawn up as the visitors were escorted to their carriages by waiting Army officers.

Now, the imposing procession started up the steep slope, at a little past mid-afternoon.

Just as the head of the line reached the flat plain above, most of the members of the Board of Visitors felt tempted to clap their hands to their ears. For a second detachment of artillery, waiting on the plain, now thundered forth the official artillery salute to the visitors.

One of these visitors, a member of the national House of Representatives, who had served with distinction in the Civil War, having then risen to the grade of major general of volunteers, looked out over the plain, then at the stalwart cadets behind, with moist eyes. He had been a cadet here in the late fifties. He was now too old to fight, but all the ardor of the soldier still burned in his veins!

Yet only a moment did the line of carriages pause at the plain.

Then the members of the Board were carried on to the West Point Hotel, where the best quarters had been reserved for such as were not to be personal guests of officers on the post.

During the brief wait at the station, Cadet Captain Prescott, standing before the company that he had commanded during this year, caught a brief glimpse of a familiar figure——his mother. By chance Mrs. Prescott had journeyed to West Point on the same train.

Yet not a chance did Dick get for a word with his mother until long after. He was almost frenzied with eagerness for word of Laura, and this his mother would have, in some form, but he must wait until all the duties of the day had been performed and leisure had come to him.

Mrs. Prescott, on catching sight of her boy, felt a sudden, exultant throb in her mother heart. Then she stepped quickly back, fearful of attracting her lad's attention at a moment when he must give his whole thought to his soldier duties.

"My noble, manly boy!" thought the mother, with moistening eyes.

"I wonder if I do wrong to think him the noblest of them all?"

Dick had caught that one swift glance, but did not again see his mother, for his eyes were straight ahead.

When the time came for his particular company to wheel and swing into the now moving line of gray, Mrs. Prescott heard his measured, manly voice: "Fours left—march!"

When the last company of cadets had fallen into line, Mrs. Prescott was one of the two dozen or so civilians who fell in at some distance to the rear, climbing the slope behind the moving line of gray. Wholly absorbed in the corps, Dick's mother had forgotten to board the stage that would have carried her to the hotel.

After the visitors had been left at the hotel, the corps marched away. Barely half an hour later, however, the two battalions again marched on to the plain. Then the most fascinating, the most inspiring of all military ceremonies was gone through with by the best body of soldiery in the world. The cadets of the United States Military Academy went through all the solemnity of dress parade. It is a sight which, once seen at West Point, can never be forgotten by a lover of his flag.

One bespectacled young spectator there was who found his breath coming in quick, sharp gasps as he looked on at this magnificent display. He was tall, yet with a slight stoop in his shoulders. His face was covered with a bushy, sandy beard. He was neither particularly well nor very badly dressed, and would have attracted little attention in any crowd.

Yet this stranger was not looking on a new sight. For nearly four years it had been as the breath of life to him.

Stoop-shouldered as a matter of disguise, and with beard and spectacles adding to his security from recognition, this slouching young man bent most of his gaze upon the stalwart, erect figure of Cadet Captain Prescott.

"You drove me out of here! You cheated me of all the glory of this career, Prescott! Have you been fool enough to think that I'd forget—that I could forget? You are close to your diploma, now—but before that moment arrives I shall find the way to spoil your chances of a career in the Army. And I can get away again without anyone recognizing in me the man who was once known as Cadet Jordan, of the first class!"

Yes; it was Jordan, back at West Point, sure of escaping recognition, and bent on a desperate errand of wrecking Dick Prescott's promising career.

But Dick performed all his duties through that dress parade conscious only of the glory of the soldier's life. He thought he had caught a fleeting glimpse of his mother once, in the crowd, as his company executed a wheeling, and he was happy in what he knew her happiness to be.

Then, when it was all over, and the corps again marched from the field, Mrs. Prescott, who knew the ways of West Point, went and stood at the edge of the grassy plain, nearly opposite the north sally-port. Five minutes after the last of the corps had marched in under the port, Dick, his dress uniform changed for the fatigue, came out with bounding step and crossed the road.

Wholly unashamed, he passed his arms around his mother, gave her a big hug, several kisses, and then, hat in hand, turned to stroll with her under the trees.

"Dad couldn't come, I'm afraid?" Dick asked in disappointment.

"He had to stay and look after the store, you know, Dick, my boy. But the store will be closed two days this week, for your father is coming on here to see you graduate. Nothing could keep him away from that."

"And how is everyone at home? How is Laura?" Dick asked eagerly.

"She will be here in time for the graduation hop," replied Mrs. Prescott. "She told me she had seen you so far through your West Point life, that she would feel uneasy over not being here to see the last move of all. Dick, do you mind your mother asking you a question? You used to care especially for Laura Bentley, did you not?"

"Why, mother?" asked Prescott with a sudden sinking at heart.

Lounging against the other side of a tree that Prescott and his mother were passing, the disguised Jordan was close enough to hear.

What he heard seemed to deepen the scowl of hatred on his face; but mother and son were soon out of ear shot, and the miserable Jordan slunk away.

CHAPTER XXII

CADET PRESCOTT COMMANDS AT SQUADRON DRILL.

The Military Academy found itself in a whirling round of recitations and drills, arranged for the delight of the Board of Visitors.

There were other hundreds of spectators at first, and thousands later, to see all that was going on, for there are hosts of citizens who know what inspiring sights are to be found at West Point in Graduation Week.

"Mr. Prescott is directed to report at the office of the commandant of cadets."

This order was borne by a soldier orderly immediately after breakfast on the day before graduation.

"Mr. Prescott," said the commandant, when the tall, soldierly looking cadet knocked, entered and saluted, "you will take command at the cavalry squadron drill, which takes place at three this afternoon."

Dick's heart bounded with pleasure. It was an honor that could come to but one man in the first class, and he was greatly delighted that it should have fallen to him.

"Mr. Holmes will command the first troop, and Mr. Anstey the second," continued the commandant of cadets, who then rattled off the names of the cadets who would act as subalterns in the squadron.

It was a splendid detail, that of commanding the squadron in the cavalry drill——splendid because it is one of the most picturesque events of the week, and also because it calls for judgment and high ability to command.

"I must be sure to get word to mother; she mustn't miss a sight that will delight her so greatly," murmured Dick, as he hastened away to notify Greg and Anstey.

This done, he hastened off to other duties, though not without yielding much thought to the belief that Laura Bentley would be here this afternoon, since she was pledged to go with him to the graduation ball in the evening.

"Mother can be sure to see Laura, and they can see the squadron drill together," ran through Prescott's mind.

A splendid, swift bit of pontoon bridge building had been shown the visitors on the day before; one battalion had given a lively glimpse of tent pitching in perfect alignment as to company streets, and in record time.

In the forenoon, there was to be a lively battery drill, to be followed by a dizzying demonstration of the speed at which machine guns may be moved, placed in position and fired so fast that there is a hail of projectiles.

For this afternoon, the cavalry drill in squadron, and after that, infantry drill that would include a picture of infantry on the firing line. After that, the last dress parade in which the present first classmen would ever take part as cadets.

Oh, it was a stirring picture, full of all the dash, the precision and glamour of the soldier's life! The pity of it all was that every red-blooded American boy could not be there to see it all.

Just before three o'clock every man of the first class turned out through the north sallyport in the full equipment of a cavalryman. Here they halted before barracks.

Dick caught sight of four figures standing hardly more than across the road. A swift glance at the time, and Prescott stepped over the road.

"Good afternoon, mother. Good afternoon, Mrs. Bentley. And Laura and Belle——oh, how delighted I am to see you both here!"

Genuine joy shone in this manly cadet's eyes; none could mistake that.

"You did not know that Greg had invited me to the graduation ball, did you?" asked Belle Meade.

"I did not," Dick answered truthfully. "Yet I guessed it as soon as I saw you here. And you have been at the Annapolis graduation, too?"

"Why, of course!" exclaimed Belle, almost in astonishment. "And Laura went with me. That's something else you didn't know, Dick."

"I've been through the course at West Point," laughed the cadet, "and by this time I am not astonished at the number of things that I don't know."

"Dave and Dan said they had seen you only a few days ago, but they sent their love again," rattled on Miss Meade. "But I'm taking up all of the talk, and I know you're dying to talk to Laura."

Belle accompanied her words with a little gesture of one hand that displayed the flash of a small solitaire diamond set in a band of gold on the third finger of the left hand.

Dick did not need inquire. He knew that Dave Darrin had placed that ring where it now flashed.

Just then Greg came through the sally-port. In an instant he bounded across the road. He immediately took it upon himself to talk with Belle, and Dick turned to Laura with flushed face and wistful eyes.

In the first instant Miss Bentley flushed; then a sudden pallor succeeded the flush. Dick, taking her dear face as his barometer, felt a sudden indescribable sinking of his heart.

They exchanged a few words, then——-

Ta-ra-ta-ra-ta-ra-ta!

It was the bugle calling the assembly.

Swiftly Greg sprang across the road to form his troop, while Anstey formed the other.

Both acting troop leaders turned to report to Dick that their respective troops were formed.

Then Prescott, for the last time as a cadet, marched the class across the plain at swift, rhythmic tread, to where the veteran cavalry horses stood saddled and tethered.

Reaching the cavalry instructor, Prescott halted, saluted, and reported his command.

"Stand to horse!" ordered the instructor briskly. There was a dash; in another instant each cadet stood by the head of his selected mount.

"Prepare to mount!"

Each cadet seized mane and bridle, also thrusting his left foot into stirrup box.

"Mount!"

Like so many figures operated by machinery, the first classmen rose, throwing right legs over saddles, then settling down in the seat. Then, all in a twinkling, the ranks reformed.

"Mr. Prescott, take command of the squadron, sir!" rang the instructor's voice.

Dick thrilled with pleasure as he received the command with a salute. He had not looked, but he knew that those dearest to him were in the crowd beyond, looking on.

"Draw sabre!" sounded Dick's not loud but clean-cut order.

Greg and Anstey repeated the order in turn. Instantly all down the strong line naked steel leaped forth. The sabres sprang to the "carry," and the superb picture breathed of military might.

Cadet Captain Dick Prescott, well in advance, sat facing his squadron; he throbbed with a soldier's ardor at the beauty of the scene.

"Fours right!" he shouted.

"Fours right! Fours right!" sounded in the differing tones of Greg and Anstey.

"March!"

"March! March!"

Into a long column of fours, to the tune of jingling accoutrements, the squadron swung. Prescott wheeled about and rode forward at a walk. In the same instant, the bugler, a musician belonging to the Regular Army, trotted forward, then slowed down to a walk close to the young squadron commander. From that time on, all the commands were to be given by the bugle.

"Trot! March!" traveled on clear, musical notes, and the long line of young horsemen moved forward at a faster gait. There was none of the bumping up and down in saddle that disfigures the riding taught in most riding schools. These gray-clad young centaurs rode as though parts of their animals.

Straight past the canvas shelter that had been erected for the superintendent, the Board of Visitors and their ladies, swung the four platoons in magnificent order and rhythm.

Then, on the return, the young cavalrymen swept, at a gallop, by platoons, in echelon and by column of squads. This done, the cadets rode forward, baiting in line before the reviewers. Here the senior cavalry instructor rode in front and gave the command:

"Present——sabres!"

The salute to the superintendent and his guests was given with magnificent precision.

"Continue the drill, Mr. Prescott!" rang the senior instructor's voice.

Once more the line of gray and steel swept over the plain. Now, the evolutions were those of the field in war time. The charge brought cheers from a thousand throats, and a great fluttering of handkerchiefs.

Then, while three platoons halted, remaining motionless in saddle, the fourth platoon, after starting at the gallop, sheathed sabres and drew pistols.

Crack! crack! Crack! crack! It was merely mimic war, with blank ammunition, but not an onlooker escaped the impression of how much death and destruction such a line of charging, firing men might carry before them.

Now the whole squadron was in motion once more. At the sharp, clear order of the bugle the line halted. At the next peal one man in every four stood at the heads of four horses, while the other three of each four ran quickly forward, in fine though open formation.

"Halt! Kneel! Ready! Aim! At will——*fire!*"

Here was battle, real enough in everything but the fatalities. Each man on the firing line fired rapidly, several shots to the minute, though real aim was taken every time the bolt was shot forward and before the trigger was pulled. Tiny, almost invisible puffs of smoke issued from the carbine muzzles. Next, an orderly spirited, swift retreat in the face of an imaginary enemy, was made to the horses, which were mounted like a flash, and spurred away. Some horses carried double, for some of the cadets lay limp and useless, impersonating men wounded by the pursuing enemy. It was all so stirring, so grand, that the plain rang with cheers.

In an hour the drill was over, and the young cavalrymen stood under the showers or disported in the pool. Only for a few minutes, however. The infantry drill followed swiftly, after which these same men must swiftly be immaculate in white ducks and the handsome gray full-dress jackets.

Then followed dress parade, after which came supper, and the first classmen at West Point were through with the last day of full duty in gray!

CHAPTER XXIII

A WEST POINTER'S LOVE AFFAIR

With beating heart Dick Prescott presented himself at the hotel that evening, and sent up his card to Mrs. Bentley and the girls. Greg was with his chum, of course, but Greg was not in a flutter. He was to escort Belle Meade——an arrangement of chumship, for Belle wore the engagement ring of Dave Darrin, one of Greg's old High School chums.

For Dick, this was the night to which he had looked forward during four years. To-night he felt sure of his career; he was to be graduated into the Army, with a position in life fine enough for Laura to grace with him.

It was on this night, that he had determined to find out whether her heart beat for him, or whether it had already been captured by young Mr. Cameron back in the home town.

"And very likely she wouldn't think of having either of us," smiled Dick to himself. "It's easy enough for a girl to be a fellow's friend, but when it comes to selecting a husband she is quite likely to be more particular."

It was just after dark as the two young couples sauntered away from the hotel on their way to Cullum Hall.

"You young men are now sure of your Army careers," remarked Belle, as the four strolled down the road.

"As absolutely sure as one can ever be of anything," Dick responded.
"Yes, I feel positive that I am now to be an officer in the Army."

"While poor Dave has just started on a two-year cruise, and must then come back for another examination before he is sure of his commission," sighed Belle.

"The middies don't get a square deal," said Dick regretfully. "When Darrin and Dalzell were graduated, the other day, they should have been commissioned as ensigns before they were ordered to sea. Some day Congress and the people will see the injustice of it all, and the unfairness will be remedied."

How could Prescott possibly know that his commission in the Army was not yet sure?

That same sandy-bearded, bespectacled and stoop-shouldered ex-cadet Jordan was even now eyeing Dick from a little distance.

"Humph! Prescott feels mighty big at this moment!" growled the young scoundrel. "I wonder how he'll be feeling at midnight, down in cadet hospital, when the surgeons tell him he has no chance of ever being a sound man again? Confound him! I could almost find it in my heart to kill the fellow, instead of merely maiming him. But maiming will be the keener revenge. All his life hereafter Prescott will be thinking what might have been if he hadn't met me this night! Shall I leap on him when he's coming back from the hotel, after the graduation ball? No; for he'd have Holmes with him then. I'll send in word and call him out from the ball, with a message that an old schoolmate wants to see him on something most urgent. I'll have Prescott to myself, and all I need is a few seconds. I'm half as powerful again as Prescott is!"

Jordan was not at all lacking in a certain type of ferocious brute courage. As he had just boasted to himself, he was powerful enough to be able to overpower Dick in a hand-to-hand conflict, yet the scoundrel meant to attack Prescott unawares, without giving the latter a chance to defend himself.

Then, too, the sight of Laura, looking sweeter and more beautiful than she had ever appeared in her life, goaded Jordan on to greater fury.

"That is the very girl I had planned to cut Prescott out with, after he had been kicked from the service, and I was still in the uniform. But it fell out the other way about," gritted Jordan. "Prescott wears the uniform, and I've been dishonorably dropped from the rolls! Prescott, I've a double score to settle with you to-night!"

But of all this, of course, Prescott was wholly unaware.

"How much time have we to spare?" queried Dick, then glancing at his watch. "Ten minutes. Laura, will you stroll around the Hall with me and look down over the cliff at the noble old Hudson! This will be one of my last glimpses as a cadet."

Laura assented. Greg was about to follow, when Belle Meade drew him back.

"Take me inside," she urged. "I am eager to see the decorations."

"But Dick and Laura?" queried Greg.

"They're of age and can take care of themselves," smiled Miss Meade.

Dick Prescott's heart was beating, now, like a trip-hammer. Even the next day's graduation, and the entrance into the Army looked insignificant to him compared with the question of his fate that was now seething in his brain and which he must now have settled.

Two or three times he opened his lips to speak, then closed them, as the two young people stood glancing down at the river through the darkness.

"Aren't you unusually silent, Dick?" asked Laura.

"Perhaps so," he assented in a low voice. "I'm scared."

"Scared!"

"Yes; scared cold. I never knew such a fright in my life before."

"Why, what———"

"Laura, I reckon the brief, direct way of the soldier will be best. Laura, ever since we were in High School together I have loved you. Through all the years that have followed, that love has never slumbered for an instant. It has grown stronger with every passing \ week. I———"

With a little cry Laura Bentley drew back.

"I'm going right through to the end," cried Dick desperately. "Then you can throw cold water over me——if you must. Laura, I love you, and that love is nearly all of my life! I ask you to become a soldier's bride——mine!"

"And——and——is that what has scared you?" asked Laura in a very low voice.

"Yes!"

"What a pitiful coward you are, then, to be a candidate for a commission in the Army," laughed Laura Bentley softly.

"But you——you haven't answered me."

"Why, Dick, I've never had another thought, in six years, than that I loved you!"

"Laura! You love me?"

"Why, of course, Dick. What has ailed your eyes and your reasoning powers?"

With a glad cry, Prescott gathered his betrothed in his arms, claiming a lover's privilege.

Then out of an inner pocket he drew a little box, drew out a circlet of gold in which a solitaire glistened, and slipped the ring over the finger set apart for the purpose of wearing such pledges.

"And how soon, Laura——sweetheart?" he demanded eagerly.

"Now, as to that, you must act like a creature of reason," Laura laughingly insisted. "You are not yet in the Army. At first, after you do receive your commission, you must be saving and careful. It needs furniture and all those things, you see, Dick, dearest, to form the background of a home. We must wait a little while——but what sweet waiting it will be!"

"Won't it, though!" demanded Dick with fervor. "Laura, it seems to me that I must be dreaming. I can scarcely realize my great good fortune."

91

"Nor can I," replied Laura softly. "You have always been my boy knight, Dick."

As they stepped inside and approached their nearest friends, Belle murmured in Greg's ear:

"Look at the electric glow that comes from the third finger of Laura's left hand. Now, do you comprehend, booby, what a fatal mistake you would have made, had I allowed you to tag them around to the cliff?"

"Well, I'm jiggered!" gasped Cadet Holmes. "Which means that I'm petrified with delight."

"Get practical, then," chided Belle. "Take me forward to them, and we'll have the happiness of being the first to congratulate the newest arrivals in paradise!"

Two minutes later, the leader of the orchestra swung his baton. As the music pealed forth, Dick Prescott knew, for the first time in his life, the full meaning of the dance in Cullum Hall.

There were many other newly betrothed couples on the floor that happy night of the graduation ball. The air was fragrant with flowers, but there was more—-the atmosphere of new-found happiness on all sides.

Outside, in the shadow of the moonless night, a stoop-shouldered figure prowled in the near vicinity of Cullum Hall. This was Jordan, intent on guessing when would be the most favorable moment for sending in the message that should call Prescott out to his doom.

One of the watchmen, a soldier, in the quartermaster's department, belted, and with a revolver hanging therefrom in its holster, passed by and noted Jordan.

"Are you waiting for anyone, sir?" asked the watchman, halting a moment, though only in mild curiosity.

"I'm going to send a message in, after the music stops, for my cousin," replied Jordan, who knew that he must give some account of himself.

"Your cousin? A cadet?" asked the watchman.

"Oh, yes. Mr. Atterbury, of the first class," responded Jordan, giving the name of his former roommate at a venture.

"Very good, sir," replied the watchman, and passed on.

Mr. Atterbury, however, at that very moment, chanced to be standing on the further side of a tree not far distant, and with him were two other first classmen.

"Who is that fellow?" queried Atterbury in a low whisper. "I've seen him around here before this, and his voice sounds mighty familiar."

The passing watchman heard the question, so he answered: "He says he is your cousin, sir!"

"He is not my cousin," replied Atterbury with strange sternness. "And, since the fellow is here in disguise, it ought to be our business to ask him some questions. Come on, fellows!"

Atterbury strode out of the shadow, followed just a second later by "Durry" and "Doug."

The prowler's first instinct was to run, but he dare not; that would proclaim guilt.

"See here, sir," demanded Atterbury, striding straight up to the stoop-shouldered, bewhiskered one, "your name is Jordan, isn't it?"

"No!" lied the wretch, in a voice that he strove to disguise.

"Yes, it is," insisted Atterbury. "Rooming with you nearly four years, I can't be fooled with any suddenly pickled voice. Jordan, what are you doing here in disguise?"

"I don't know that my presence here is any of your business," growled the ex-cadet.

"Yes; it is," insisted Atterbury. "And you'll give us an account, too, or we'll lay hold of you and turn you over to some one official."

At that threat Jordan turned to bolt. As he did so, three cadets sprang after him. At the third or fourth bound they had hold of him and bore him, fighting, to the earth.

Even now Jordan used his splendid physique and strength in a determined, bitter struggle.

But "Durry" helped turn the fellow over, face down, and then all three sat on their catch.

"Doug," however, felt something hard. Leaping up, he made a quick search, then drew from Jordan's hip pocket a length of lead pipe wrapped in red flannel.

"Ye gods of war," gasped Douglass, "what sort of weapon is this for a former gentleman to carry?"

"Let me up," pleaded Jordan, "and I'll make a quick hike!"

"Don't you let him up, fellows," warned Douglass. "Now, whom did Jordan seek with an implement like this? There could be but one of our men—-Prescott."

"Have you anything to say, Jordan?" demanded Atterbury.

"Not a blessed word," growled Jordan, no longer attempting to disguise his voice.

"Then we have," returned "Doug."

"But you two fellows hold him until I come back."

Douglass ran over to the cliff, then, with a mighty throw, hurled the bar of lead out into the Hudson, far below. Then he darted back.

"Now, fellows," muttered Douglass in a low voice, "I'd like mighty well to turn this scoundrel over. But we don't want to put such a foul besmirchment on the class name, if we can avoid it, the night before graduation. Jordan, if we let you go, will you hike, and never stop hiking until you're miles and miles away from West Point?"

"Yes; on my honor," protested the other eagerly.

"On your—-bosh!" retorted "Doug" impatiently. "Don't spring such strange oaths on us, fellow. Let him."

"Now, Jordan, start moving, and keep it up!" Then the trio, after watching the rascal out of sight, went inside, and Douglass, at the first opportunity, warned Dick of what had happened outside in the summer darkness.

CHAPTER XXIV

CONCLUSION

The graduating exercises at West Point had finished. The Secretary of War, in the presence of the superintendent, the commandant and the members of the faculty of the United States Military Academy, flanked by the Board of Visitors, had handed his diploma to the last man, the cadet at the foot of the graduating class, Mr. Atterbury.

Dick had graduated as number thirty-four; Greg as thirty-seven. Either might have chosen the cavalry, or possibly the artillery arm of the service, but both had already expressed a preference for the infantry arm.

"The 'doughboys' (infantry) are always the fellows who see the hardest of the fighting in war time," was the way Dick put it.

Now the superintendent made a few closing remarks. These finished, the band blared out with a triumphal march, to the first notes of which the first class rose and marched out, amid cheers and hand-clapping, to be followed by the other classes.

Five minutes later the young graduates were laying aside the gray uniform for good and all. Cit. clothes now went on, and each grad. surveyed himself with some wonder in attire which was so unfamiliar.

Out in the quadrangle, for the last time, the grads. met. There, too, were the members of the classes remaining, but these latter were still in the cadet gray, and would be until the close of their own grad. days.

Hurried good-byes were said. Warm handclasps sounded on all sides. Few words were said, but there were many wet eyes.

Then some of the grads. raced for the station to board the next city-bound train.

Greg remained behind with Dick. After quitting the quadrangle, they bent swift steps toward the hotel, where awaited Mrs. Prescott, Mrs. Bentley, Laura and Belle.

Something else waited, too—a carriage, or rather, a small bus, for Dick and Greg were no longer cadets and might ride over the post in a carriage if they chose.

"It was beautifully impressive, dear," whispered Laura, referring to the graduating exercises.

"But, thank goodness, it's over, and I have my diploma in this suit case," murmured Dick grimly. "No more fearful grind, such as we've been going through for more than four years. No more tortured doubts as to whether we'll ever grad. and get our commissions in the Army. That is settled, now. And think, Laura, if I hear a bugle in the city to-morrow morning, I can simply turn over and take another nap."

"You lazy boy!" laughed Laura half chidingly.

"You spend four years and three months here, and see if you don't feel the same way about it," smiled Dick. "But I love every gray stone in these grand old buildings, just the same. West Point shall be ever dear in my memory!"

Greg's mother now came out and joined the ladies on the porch. A moment or two later Mr. Prescott and Mr. Holmes stepped out and grasped their sons' hands.

"We haven't a heap of time left if we want to catch the down-river steamboat," suggested Dick, with a glance at his watch.

So this happy little home party entered the bus, and the drive to the dock began.

They passed scores of cadets, who carefully saluted these grads.

Everyone in the party knew of the betrothal of Dick and Laura. Greg had had to stand a good deal of good-natured chaffing from his parents because he had not fared as well.

"The next girl I get engaged to," sighed Greg, "I'm going to insist on marrying instantly. Then there'll be no danger of losing her."

At the dock, Anstey, Durville, Douglass and other grads. waited, though the majority of the members of the late first class were already speeding to New York on a train that had started a few minutes earlier.

"I couldn't bear to go down by train, suh," explained Anstey in a very low voice. "I want to stand at the stern of the steamer, and see West Point's landmarks fade and vanish one by one. And I don't reckon, suh, that I shall want anyone to talk to me while I'm looking back from the stern of the boat."

"Same here," observed Greg, with what was, for him, a considerable display of feeling.

Then the boat swept in, and the West Point party went silently aboard. All made their way to the stern on the saloon deck.

That evening the class was to meet, for the last time as a whole, at one of the theaters in New York. And the late cadets would sit together, solidly, as a class.

Friends of graduates who wished would attend the theater, though in seats away from the class.

Dick and Greg's relatives and friends were all to attend. More, they were to stop at the same hotel. The next forenoon the ladies would attend to some shopping. Then the reunited party would journey back to Gridley.

A dozen or so West Point graduates stood at the stern of the swift river steamer. The captain of the craft, a veteran in the river service, knew something of how these young men just out of the gray felt. For the first five miles down the river the swift craft went at half speed. Then, suddenly, full speed ahead was rung on the engine-room bell, and the craft went on under greatly increased headway.

"Well, gentlemen," murmured Anstey, moving around and walking slowly forward, "the United States Military Academy is the grandest alma mater that a fellow could possibly have. I'm glad to be through, glad to be away from West Point, but I shall journey reverently back there any time when I have any leisure in this bright part of the good old world."

How sweet the joys of the great metropolis! Yet these joys would have palled had our travelers remained there too long. The following afternoon they were again journeying toward what is, after all, the one real spot on earth—-home!

Gridley well-nigh went wild over its returning West Pointers—-though now West Pointers no longer.

One of Dick Prescott's first tasks was to go proudly to Dr. Bentley, to state that he had had the wonderful good fortune to win Laura's heart, and to ask whether her father had any objection.

"Objection, Dick?" beamed the good old physician. "Why, lad, for years I've been hoping—-yes, praying that you and Laura would have this good fortune.

Wherever you may be stationed in the world, you'll let our daughter come back to us once in a while, I hope."

Dick solemnly promised, whereat Dr. Bentley smiled.

"That's all nonsense, Dick," laughed Laura's father. "I know, in my own heart, that you're going to be as good a son to mother and me as you have been to your own parents. God bless you both!"

A new lot of High School boys Dick and Greg found in Gridley, but the new crop seemed to be fully as promising as any that Dick and Greg could remember in their own old High School days when Dick & Co. had flourished.

A fortnight, altogether, Dick and Greg enjoyed in the good old home town, hallowed to them by so many memories.

Then one morning each received a bulky official envelope bearing the imprint of the War Department at Washington.

How their eyes glistened, then moistened, as each young West Point grad. drew out of the envelope the parchment on which was written his commission as a second lieutenant of United States infantry.

More, their request had been granted. They had been assigned to the same regiment—-the forty-fourth.

Their instructions called for them to start within forty-eight hours, and to wire acknowledgment of orders to Washington.

The Forty-fourth United States Infantry was at that time in the far West, in a country that at times teemed with adventure for Uncle Sam's soldiers.

Here we must take leave of Lieutenant Dick Prescott and of Lieutenant Greg Holmes, United States Army, for their cadet days are over and gone.

Readers, however, who wish to meet these sterling young Americans again, and who would also like to renew acquaintance with two former members of Dick & Co., Tom Reade and Harry Hazelton, will be able to do so in Volume Number Five of the *Young Engineers' Series*, entitled: "*The Young Engineers On The Gulf.*"

In this very interesting volume the young engineers and the young Army officers will be found to have some very startling adventures together.

Readers will also be able to learn more of the careers of Dick Prescott and Greg Holmes, as Army officers, in the "*Boys Of The Army Series*." Some of their campaigns will be described very fully, for these splendid young officers served as officers and instructors of the "*Boys of the Army*."

THE END

CPSIA information can be obtained at www.ICGtesting.com
Printed in the USA
LVOW05s1749220114

370539LV00039B/1863/P